THE CURSE OF TECUMSEH

TECUMSEH

——And Other Stories——

RYAN ROBINSON

Word Art Publishing
9350 Wilshire Blvd
Suite 203, Beverly Hills, CA 90212
www.wordartpublishing.com
Phone: 1 (888) 614 - 1370

Published by Word Art Publishing

ISBN: Paperback   978-1-955070-12-6
       Hardback   978-1-955070-13-3
       Ebook   978-1-955070-14-0

TABLE OF CONTENTS

This book is dedicated to:

Kay Klem and all her students.
Especially, JoAnn, Eleanor, Penny, Bob, and Vivian,
for all the help they gave getting me started.
To Hal and Jan for sticking with me.
To Tree, for making it much better.
And a special hats off to the Secret Service, tough job.

THE CURSE OF TECUMSEH

S ometimes when an ordinary guy is about to make the most important decision in his life he needs to get out by himself and walk around. It's a precious opportunity to clear the mind. It turned into the ideal evening to escape formality and responsibilities for a soul-searching stroll. Summer lingered during the day, and a light jacket at night felt cozy. My cluttered mind and I moved toward the lights.

You wouldn't call this Oklahoma town small; and yet it didn't have the look or size of a modern city. It looks the same as I remembered it as a child. Walking down Main Street with my parents and ridding my bicycle to the stores with my friends. Perhaps the storefront lights were brighter. I found downtown at that magic time of dark blue twilight and Venus' un-twinkling gleam.

Hudson Appliance on Main Street still left a TV turned on in the window, a holdover of a less hectic time. An old, leather faced man, with his thick, silver-gray hair tied back, arms folded across his chest, watched the images. A smiling, perfect blonde recited the news about the politics of the day. Through a small speaker above the window, she talked of the pending primary race.

"A nice picture for a set of that size," the man said.

"Yes, it is," I replied. I didn't realize that Native Americans were such connoisseurs of picture quality. "What do you think of the upcoming primary campaign between Zimmer, Peterson and the others? Or are you one of those people sticking with the President?"

"What did the New York Times say about him? More unpopular than Nixon, but no evidence to impeach," he said with a smile.

"What about the others? Do you think any of them would make a good candidate?" I asked, wondering if

I had annoyed him too much, but I was desperate for an answer.

"It doesn't matter who becomes president," he said and turned his attention back to the news.

"How can you say that? The president is the most powerful person in the country . . . in the world." Why was this man so cavalier about this country? "We should do everything we can to elect the right person. And you should be especially concerned. Zimmer has supported the Native American Nations Resolution; and Peterson has opposed it. And the President . . ."

"Has never heard about it," he chimed in.

We both had a quiet laugh. His worn dusty blue jeans and wrinkled face could not conceal his bright intelligent eyes. I stuck out my hand.

"My name is John."

"I'm Theodore Graywolf. My friends call me Teddy." This Native American had a firm handshake.

"It's good to meet you. But I have got to ask you if you think the Presidency is a meaningless job?"

"Don't get me wrong, John. I have the highest regard for that position. But because of The Curse, It's who gets elected Vice President that's important this year."

"Curse? What curse?"

"The Curse of Tecumseh."

"I've never heard of that one," I said, quickly searching my brain for everything I knew about that historic Indian chief.

"It's simple enough. A President elected in a year ending in zero will die a sudden or violent death while in office. And since this next election year is 2020, it makes the position of Vice President the one we should care about."

This can't be right, but he looked me straight in the eyes with a glint of a smile that comes with knowing something I didn't. I had no reason to doubt his sincerity. And yet, I couldn't openly accept his statement, hitting too close to home and far from reality.

"I've never heard of such a thing."

"You haven't?"

"If I did, it never went by that name. Are you sure and not mistaken?"

"Yes," he said simply, and then started to rub his chin. "It started with William Henry Harrison, elected in 1840. He died after only a month in office. That's probably why we don't hear more about him. Everyone knows about Abraham Lincoln, elected in 1860. The election of 1880 went to James Garfield. He died after six months in office, shot by a mentally disturbed office seeker."

"I thought only the insane could apply. Sorry," I said. "You seem to know your history well."

"Thank you. I've always studied the past. So my people can learn from it."

"Excuse me. I've interrupted you. This is interesting. It seems that this is happening every twenty years. After 1880, the next time would be 1900," I said, zipping up my wind breaker. The sky had darkened and this night would bring a chill, but I needed to hear this.

"Yes. McKinley was elected in 1896, and then again in 1900. He died, shot by an anarchist, in September of 1901."

"Anarchists have been getting a bad rap ever since," I couldn't resist saying.

"This is true. That brings us to Warren Harding, elected in 1920. Shortly after returning from Alaska in 1923, he became ill, and died. And while he had been sick for much of his time in office, Roosevelt sudden death during his fourth term still shocked the nation."

"Yes, if I remember correctly he was elected in 1940 for his third term."

"That's right. The next zero year is 1960. That would be JFK's election. Most people know about that one."

"It's interesting how Lincoln and Kennedy stand out in our minds, and the others seem vague."

"I've noticed that, when I talk to people. It's funny how they're a hundred years apart." Teddy stuffed his hands into the pockets of his denim jacket. "Do you know the only exceptions to The Curse? As with rules, there is always that special case when it doesn't apply." He looked at me again with that knowing smile.

"Ronald Reagan, elected 1980, didn't die in office," I said, pointing my hand at him. I have been told that I should try to eliminate that unconscious habit.

"Even though he didn't die, the assassination attempt came close. The bullet deflected off a rib and came to rest in Reagan's lung. Too close to the heart, if you ask me. Especially when you consider the bullet used—a .22 caliber Devastator, designed to explode on impact. Yet it didn't go off, and he lived."

"What do you think happened? Why didn't he fall under this curse?" I couldn't believe I was talking like this curse could be true.

"I don't know. Perhaps he did. He was that far from death." Teddy held up his thumb and index finger a half inch apart. "Perhaps the Great Sprit chose to spare him. Still, Reagan felt the sting. Remember that three other people were seriously wounded in that attempt. Then of course, there's the election of 2000, everybody knows nothing happened then. That is the exception that proves the rule."

My thoughts could not help but relive the memory of that day in high school. We all sat in class, and watched the inauguration of Bush on the monitor with the rest of the world as it happened.

"So all the Presidents that die in office are elected in a year that ends in zero?"

"No. One President didn't fall on a zero. Zachary Taylor, elected in 1848, died suddenly from cholera, after one year and four months in office."

"He was the only one? I though for sure there would be more."

"No, just him," said Teddy, a smile spread crossed his weathered face.

"This is all very fascinating. It looks like there is a pattern. But a curse? I can't believe that. And how could these events be caused by Tecumseh? Are you saying he actually put some kind of voodoo spell on the country?"

"I don't know about a spell," he spoke knowingly. "But it is an old and interesting story."

My curiosity stirred even deeper, I needed to find out what supported this wild notion of mystic intervention into the worlds' most logical and fair political system. I couldn't let this old sage escape until I learned the truth, even if I didn't believe it. A cold shiver ran through me.

"If I buy you a cup of coffee, would you tell me the whole story?" I asked, pointing to the café down at the street corner. He looked like he could use a warm cup and so could I.

"I've been told they have excellent pie," he countered.

"I think we should find out. You know, to put those rumors to rest."

*   *   *

We sat on the plastic seats next to the window. The sound of sliding dishes, chitchat, and the aroma from the special of the day filled our senses. He held his cup with both hands savoring its warmth and smell, as if the coffee alone kept life flowing through his veins.

"Tecumseh had been trying to gather and unite all the tribes in the region together, to stand up against the American encroachment. He had achieved some success in forming a confederacy of tribes. I think it is that for which Tecumseh is best known. All went well until he and his brother, a Shawnee prophet named Tenskwatawa, were defeated at Tippecanoe in 1811. Can you guess the territorial governor's name?"

"William Henry Harrison," I said, making the connection. "*Tippecanoe and Tyler too* was his slogan in his 1840 champion."

"That's right. Tyler was Harrison's running mate. Harrison also destroyed their village and forced the Shawnee to move farther west."

"I'll give you this much, Tecumseh had motive. I'm sure he had determination. But could he inflict a curse?" My doubts were growing.

Teddy released the strangle hold on his coffee mug, and we turned our attention to the pie, just delivered.

"Most of these facts are so much surface history. The kind of stuff you can pull off any web site," Teddy said, looking back at me with dark, rock-steady eyes searching for some unknown response. He didn't look like the kind of person who is comfortable with the web. "Encyclopedias talk of effects, not always the root cause."

"You mean the mystical stuff?" I said, my mouth half full of apple pie.

"Yes. It's the fabric of myths and legends." An otherworldly smile touched his eyes and face.

"I may not believe them, but I do want to hear the story," I said, almost begging. "Please continue."

"Most of the tribes accepted defeat and made peace with the Americans—Tecumseh's cause forgotten. Tecumseh needed to show them a powerful sign. The New Madrid earthquakes started in the early morning of December 16, 1811. A terrifying noise rumbled from the earth. Trees toppled, rocks cracked open, rivers dried up, streams gushed forth where none had been, settlers were thrown from their beds, earthen jars shattered, and choking clouds of dust rose from sunken pits in the earth. Near the Kentucky-Tennessee border, a massive section of ground sank in the shape of a foot. Water flooded in to form what is now called Reelfoot Lake. Tens of thousands of acres were ravaged. And that was just the first of four earthquakes. Powerful were the signs from Tecumseh."

I listened to his tale with the eagerness of a little child. Teddy's voice became musical describing the destruction, of streams changing course, of rivers running backwards, the settlers' fears, and the powerful medicine of the Shawnee chief.

"On February 13, 1812 the last of the great signs struck. They said it lasted an hour, causing more damage than the other three combined and covering more than a million square miles, 16 times bigger that the San Francisco quake of 1906. No earthquake had ever been reported in this region before, and no scientific explanation could be given for their occurrence. But the warriors understood, and they gathered up their weapons to fight the war predicted by the powerful Tecumseh."

Teddy turned his head, breaking his spell, yet holding my attention.

"I could use more coffee," he said to a passing waitress.

After we both had our cups refilled, Teddy continued.

"On the eve of battle, Tecumseh sat before a fire surrounded by the stars, the earth, and his warriors.

He listened to their voices, talking among themselves about the upcoming fight with the Americans. He had been quiet, neither boasting nor lamenting; then Tecumseh stood. All became respectfully silent. He announced that '*on the morrow we will be in their smoke,*' referring to the guns of their enemy."

"*My children,*" he said, "*hear me well. Tomorrow we go into our final battle with the Americans. In this battle I will be killed.*"

"Then he gave away all his weapons, rank, and ornamentation that would identify him. He kept only his favorite war club. Then he called for his brother-in-law. Tecumseh took the ramrod of his rifle," Teddy picked up a soda straw from the table.

"He handed the rod to his brother-in-law," and said, "*When you see me fall, fight your way to my side and strike my body.*" Reaching over with the straw, Teddy tapped my hand and continued, "*four times with this rod,*". Teddy held it between us at eye level for effect. "*If you do so, I will then arise, with my life renewed and charmed against further harm, I will lead you to victory.*"

Teddy put down the metaphor, and picked up his coffee. He savored a long sip. I could barely contain myself.

"Well, what happened?" He had me at the cliff and I needed to know.

"General Harrison's army killed Tecumseh. His brother-in-law died before he did. So he couldn't tap him with a ramrod. Tecumseh did not leap up, and didn't drive the white man from the land. After the battle, when everyone had gone, warriors from his tribe snuck back. They retrieved his body. Then took him to a secret place, far from where he fell. On the edge of a clear creek, under the branches of a young tree, they laid him in the ground."

"The Shawnee believe that Tecumseh will come again. In the hour of the second coming, there will be *one town of towns*. It will mark the end of strife, wars, and contention among all Indian tribes. Then the celebration will consummate all that the Great Spirit intends for His red children."

"That's a wonderful story, and you are a great story teller, but it doesn't say there is a curse. I think he's confined by the same laws of nature as you and I."

"Tecumseh once said, *As to boundaries, the Great Spirit knows no boundaries, nor will his red children acknowledge any.*"

≈ 13 ≈

"I'm sorry, but I still can't buy it. I don't believe in The Curse," I said, confidently.

"Neither did the nine presidents who fell under it," he replied, his dark eyes cold and serious.

"Teddy, I have truly enjoyed your stories and your company, but I must be on my way."

"If you don't mind, John, I'm going to finish this cup of coffee, before I move on."

* * *

Walking back to my parents' home where I was staying, I had a lot to think about. How could that old man be right? I couldn't accept the idea of a curse. However, nine points of fact, occurring every twenty years had compelling logic that couldn't be ignored. I could no more turn my back on the chilling facts than the cold air of the night.

Do you believe in coincidence?

"Sir, you were told not to go off by yourself under any circumstance," the young man in a dark suit said, after talking into his watch.

"That's too bad. That might be the last walk I ever take by myself. I needed it," I replied, stepping around another agent in a dark suit and onto the back porch.

"I tried to tell them you'd be all right," my wife said, meeting me at the door, and taking my jacket.

I stepped into the old familiar house, smelling the friendly aroma, hearing the squeaky floor. I could see the light of the TV down the hall where my parents were, no doubt.

"Peterson called twice while you were out. She wants a decision," my secretary said, handing me slips of paper I had learned to anticipate. She folded her small hands and waited. She and my wife were the only campaign people I had brought on this trip to see my parents.

"Of course she does. I'm going up to the bedroom. I don't want to be disturbed. I'll make the call from there."

It didn't take but a few minutes to pull down the facts, or what Teddy called 'surface history'. I couldn't find any inaccuracies in his stories. This evening had been unsettling and disturbing. The truth and I made the call.

"Jessica Peterson? Zimmer here. I can still beat you in the primaries."

"I'm not so sure, John."

"I think so. However, I'm going to accept your offer anyway. I will drop out of the primary race, and run on the party ticket as the vice-presidential candidate."

"I'm glad to hear you say that. We don't agree on everything, but this is going to be one hell of a team to beat. The President doesn't have a chance. Why don't we have our press people make the announcement around ten? Then we can talk tomorrow to work out the details."

"That sounds good."

"You know, John, I think you made the right decision."

"I know I did."

*　*　*

Two men walked down the neon-lit streets of the Oklahoma town and stopped beside an old, rugged faced man with gray hair and his arms folded over his chest. They watched a TV in the appliance store window. A smiling perfect blonde recited the news of the day.

"Has the Gray Wolf chanted his tale of wonder?" the taller of the new arrivals asked.

"Yes, my brother, I told him the story. I feel very good about it. There is to be an announcement about the two candidates at ten this evening. It should be what we hoped for. Zimmer's sympathy for our cause and the Resolution will strengthen our position in this upcoming election more than at any other time in history."

After a while the youngest of the three turned to the others with a sober face, and addressed the older men with conviction.

"This is a nice picture for a set of this size," he said. They all agreed.

END

AUTHORS COMMENTS

I first herd of the curse when I was in the Army. A buddy of mine told me about it and has bothered me ever since. I wrote this story in January of 1998. In December of 2018 I revised it to better conform to the times.

The facts sated in the story are as correct as I can tell, but the story is fiction.

I hope you can understand why I find this story so disturbing. The real question is, did President Reagan break the spell by not dying or was President Bush truly the exception? This may not be the end of it. Is there more to come? The Presidential election of 2020 may be very eventful.

I don't know when you are reading this, but you can check history, either in the future or the past and see how it all turned out.

MAKE LIKE THE
GREEN PANTHER

Yet again, we've hurried up . . . and now we were waiting. The only noise came from the soft murmur of the guys' idle chitchat. Some were smoking. The deep blue sky of dusk overshadowed and dominated everything. My eyes fixed on the view of the sky. A gentle breeze brushed my face, and the voices drifted into nothingness. Only a single light bulb over the Command Bunker disturbed the evening.

Beyond the wire, a fire snake appeared above the horizon. The tracers started from nowhere, moving to the left and downward. Then it stopped. The straight red line of living embers shimmered and flowed in the persistent silence. From where the glowing ribbon came, its tail suddenly raced into the void at its head and disappeared. The invisible beast that belched the fire made no sound as it left.

"Wow, a gun ship dumping a load," Anderson spoke, shattering the mood.

If there could be any beauty in the act of destruction, I just saw it. The term Spook Ship is underrated.

As a no-name Second Lieutenant approached from the bunker, a voice in the crowd brought us to attention.

"At ease. Listen up. The password for tonight is CAMBRIDGE. Don't forget it. You've all been briefed, and you know your bunker assignments. The trucks will be here to take you out in a few minutes. As soon as you get to the bunkers, report in. One more thing— Don't be screwing up out there. Don't be shooting at shadows. If you see something, call it in before you do anything. That's all."

Shortly after this stirring speech, a three-quarter-ton arrived to take us to our duty for the night. We climbed into the back.

"Some of the guys were talkin'," Anderson said, pleased with himself to be letting us in on his newfound gossip. "They say sometimes you can see wild deer come right up to the wire. I tell ya', if I see a deer tonight, I'm baggin' it." To emphasize his words, he pointed to the ground.

Everyone ignored him.

The desert like terrain was void of anything tall. A road, set in a wide, shallow trench, ran around Long Behn's perimeter. A second ditch, one step down and just as wide, ran in front of the bunkers. Those bunkers where sandbag-covered boxes thrusting up out of the landscape spaced every hundred meters, like weathered butte in a desert valley. The only thing beyond that, were coils of barbed wire and Charley.

My unit, Fifth LEM, manned two bunkers every night, 53B and 54B. As my first turn at perimeter guard and having just made E5, that made me the bunker commander of 54B.

My sense of dread intensified when the truck stopped. I didn't want to do this, but Anderson, Smith, and I got out. As we made our way along the short, narrow path to the back door, I longed to be a White

Elephant Gypsy somewhere else doing calibration (what I'd been trained to do).

The inside of the bunker, roughly ten by ten, held two bunks along the back wall, an ammo locker on the left, an eight-inch firing step across the front, and a shelf for the field phone on the right. This was all the furniture the space could handle.

Opening death's cornucopia, the two-foot cube ammo locker, we removed the M79 grenade launcher, some H.E. rounds, and several M16 magazine bandoleers. Anderson took a box of thirty-caliber, and fed a belt into the machine gun. Smith mounted the starlight scope on his weapon. I placed the little green claymore detonators next to where the primer cord ran inside, and then made the call to the Duty Officer.

"Hey!" Smith said. "There's someone down there."

We looked out through the chicken wire on the left side. Two soldiers stood next to the claymores.

Anderson put his helmet back on and made for the door. "I'll go," I said, picking up my M16, "You count the ammo. I don't want anyone saying we took any."

A jeep parked on the road behind the bunker hadn't been there when we arrived. Had we been so busy that we didn't hear or notice them? This wasn't good.

As I approached, the taller of the two turned and glared at me. He didn't look happy. Why was he there? What was that password? Should I salute him? After all, he was a captain.

"This is terrible. Why haven't you taken care of this?" So goes formality.

"Take care of what, Sir?"

"I want all the primer cord replaced immediately."

"What seems to be the problem, Sir?" I had never seen primer cord before. How would I know good from bad?

"Look at it. The sheathing is cracked. It's exposed. I want it taken care of right away."

As the Captain and his "friend" moved off toward their jeep, I bent down to examine one of the veins running from the bunker down to the killing ditch. The sheer outer casing had partially peeled off, leaving the stark white core open to the elements.

I went back inside to make another call. "There was a Captain here. He says the primer cord on all the claymores is damaged."

"So?"

"He wants it fixed right away."

"Who the hell is he?"

"I don't know."

"You can tell him where to stick it," the voice said, with familiar disgust.

"Look. I don't want to get into trouble. I'm just passing on what I was ordered to do."

"All right, it's in the log," he said. The meaning was clear: Don't bother us.

(Click)

I stuffed the handset back into the field phone, hoping the call would cover us.

Boredom settled over us. Smith's quiet balanced out Anderson's incessant talk. Anderson was the type of guy that had to tell you about all his inconveniences in life, whether or not you wanted to hear it. And he did it while lying on the bottom bunk. Smith, on the other hand, sat on the ammo locker and only said things that were meaningful or relevant. None of this was new to me. You see all types in the Army, some good, some bad and everything in between.

The road running behind the bunkers had lights mounted on poles, but they only made vehicles on the road dimly visible. A jeep pulled up and stopped. We had little time to react.

"I'll go," Smith said. Putting on his helmet, he picked up an M16 and walked out the back.

"Get up," I said to Anderson.

Smith stopped the driver half way up the path, starting in on the password formalities. Was Anderson asleep?

"Hey, get up," I repeated, shaking his arm.

"Huh?" Anderson sat upright, shook his head, then stood up.

Smith reentered, followed by a First Lieutenant.

"Were you sleeping?" the Lieutenant asked, shooting Anderson a knowing look.

"Aaaah, no. I was just resting."

"You're not supposed to be in the bunks."

"Well, I understood one guy was to be standing and looking; another to be sitting and resting; and another lying down and resting."

"No. Everyone is up, everyone is watching the perimeter, and no one rests. Is that clear?" he asked, his tone fiery without shouting.

"Yes, Sir," we all replied.

He turned and left. We watched the jeep travel down the road then stop at the next bunker. At least we weren't being picked on. The full realization hit me why there are three men in a bunker: one to watch the front, one to cover your back, and one to be a jerk. Anderson lay back down.

Again the familiar quiet, dimness, and boredom of guard duty settled in. The talk tapered off sharply with Anderson resting. I began to think that this may turn out all right after all.

*   *   *

"Hey, Robinson, there's something out there," Smith said, coming alert and standing on the firing step. "It's a cat."

I picked up Smith's M16, and flipped the small toggle switch with my thumb. The high-pitched whine whispered in my ear as I looked through the scope. In a bath of amplified green light, a panther walked. The big green cat's shoulders pistoned up and down. He strolled down the incline from the right, toward the claymores, calmly moving his head from side to side, his tongue lying between the two lower fangs.

The hollow darkness of his eyes searched the ground belonging to him, as if he was at home, and it wasn't ours to fight over.

"Let me see," Anderson said.

I relinquished the scope. You could just make out the shadowy form with the naked eye.

"I'm going to shoot him—blast him right here."

"You can't do that," Smith said.

"Yeah, I'll bag him." Anderson's fingers twitched on the pistol grip.

"NO," I shouted, "you will not shoot him."

"Come on, I have him in my sights. I'll just pull the trigger."

"You can't fire without permission."

"Then I'll call it in, and get permission." He put down the rifle and moved to the field phone.

Smith took his turn to look through the starlight. "Wow," he finally said.

"There's a panther out on the perimeter, and I'm requesting permission to shoot it." Anderson had come down another notch—to third class idiot. "Aaaah, yes Sir. But Sir . . ."

"You want another look?" Smith turned to me.

"Thanks."

I tried to look for any kind of markings, but there weren't any, just the outline. The green neon-etched cat slowly moved up the slope, and meandered back over the embankment. Then he was gone, dissolving into the night. Only the impact remained. I will never forget his momentary defiance of our presence. Surrounded by all ugliness, he'd brought the gift of surreal beauty.

The incident occupied most of my thoughts for the rest of the uneventful night. In the morning, with bunker duty over, we were all lined up outside the perimeter to sweep the area we had guarded the night before. We found a spent flair canister, and some RVNs policing up brass. But I looked for something else. My eyes strained to see prints, tracks, or any sign that a big cat had been through there. I found nothing, but knew that phantom owned the sandy soil we walked.

When we got back to the Fifth LEM, I climbed out of the three-quarter ton, and moved toward the C.O. and the armory. The breath I took said something unmistakable. It felt and smelled of Thursday. In the morning the air came with the heavy odor from the burning latrine cans of diesel fuel and shit.

A couple of hoochs down, I heard Bob Dylan asking me how do I feel.

In front of a half-burred fifty-five-gallon drum of dirt, I slid back the bolt of my M16 and asked myself how I felt. I clenched the pistol grip tightly, stretched out my arm to full length. And, yes, I did feel like there was no direction home. I took a deep breath and held it and pulled the trigger. "Click," the weapon cleared. My direction was clear and the future was known but not complete.

I presented my weapon to the armory.

Bob Dylan had a way of making you look at things sideways. And just as sure as Thursday, I knew I would be all right. I knew that home is the direction. And someday, I too, would make like the Green Panther and walk proudly on my own ground; but not today.

END

AUTHORS COMMENTS

This story is true. The names and password have been changed to protect the . . . Not really. It's because I forgot them. But I did leave the charter's personalities the same.

Other than that, it's pretty much what happened. It was a long and spooky night. And yes, I was more afraid of the officer's harassment then Charley attacking. That's a moment in my life I will never forget.

And Bob Dylan never sounded so poignant.

BEST FRIEND

The small band of brutal scavengers grabbed the only food he had seen for the last three days, leaving him with gashes in his leg and arm. The bleeding was bad. In the dark, cold, and terrifying depths of the old Lagrange point colony, thousands of kilometers above the Moon, Charles Tailor needed a friend.

"What did they do, Charley? Look's bloody bad. That red stuff is coming out, and not going back in. We need more help than what your buddy, Nicholi, can give. That's for sure. And to do more than a shave, bath and replace these tattered clothes. I know where to get you fixed up, but we got to go there, and soon."

"I'm afraid. I don't want to go. If someone sees me, they will hurt me again. I'm safer here, Nicholi. Leave me alone. All I need is rest and some Rems."

"No can do, Charley-my-boy."

**"To die, to sleep -
No more - and by a sleep to say we end
The heartache, and the thousand natural shocks
That flesh is heir to."**

"We have to move, now. We'll take shaft FORTY-EIGHT. It's a shortcut. Time is not our friend tonight, Charley. That's it, move the leg and stand up. Over that way to the entrance."

"It hurts, Nicholi," the wounded man screamed into the darkness as he put pressure on his foot.

The once heavily used corridor of the space colony was deserted. The only exceptions were trash, dirt, and the occasional Scavenger, like himself. The shaft labeled FORTY-EIGHT went into the inner workings of the habitat. Water, sewage, and power lines were at the end of the black void. With his right hand, Charley held his blood-soaked arm. At the entrance, lingered the odor of decaying filth.

"I can't see anything. I'm too afraid. I haven't seen Scott or Richard or Laura for so long a time. Evil things are down there, and they take people away. I won't go in."

"You must, this is the quickest way. We'll take it nice and easy. Put your hand on the right sidewall, and follow it until the first turn. Be careful where you step, Charley. And ignore all the sounds."

Their progress was slow and the smells got better, then worse. The trembling hand that timidly touched the side of the tunnel felt its way over conduit, sticky slime, pipes, and objects that moved. Then suddenly, nothing.

"What happened? There's no wall. What do I do? Nicholi where are you?" Charley said, collapsing onto the floor.

"Calm down, I'm right here. We just reached the turn, it's not much farther."

At the end of what seemed like a day of bad dreams, Charley found his hands clutching a metal ladder. A faint light from somewhere showed a section of rungs above his head. The ladder rose into murkiness.

Many places in the space habitat, the gravity changed as you moved from one point to another. Charley couldn't tell if the ladder went up or down.

"I can't do it - I'm scared - I'm tired. Go away, and let me die. It hurts too much."

Nicholi ran a bloody hand through his matted hair. "Remember what happened during the tour on the Catchers Mitt. The Tycho accelerator had shot up ninety-eight tons of lunar rock. Coming in at three hundred clicks, it hit what . . . off by just a few meters. The canister went right where it shouldn't have. It felt like space itself ripping apart. Rock and dirt went everywhere, the Mitt spun out of control. With half its systems dead, only chaos knew what was going on that day. You had two broken legs, Charley. People are breathing now because you did what needed to be done. There were many heroes that day, and you were one of them."

"A break is more painful in zero-G isn't it?" Continued, Nicholi. "You can't lie down and relax. You're in constant motion and every movement is agony. You turn north, and the leg wants to drift south. During that time you conquered the pain. So don't snivel and complain to me. I know better. Get on that ladder."

Holding onto the ladder with one hand, he moved the good foot up to the next rung, and started his journey. The pain wasn't as bad as his ordeal on the Mitt, so long ago.

What happened to that young, excited, and wide-eyed adventurer that came here to build a future? How could things have changed so much? When did he trade eagerness and courage, for slovenly and cowardice? Why couldn't he be more like Nicholi? *I was like him, once.*

Charley continued up the ladder, and thought about his life in the—a village in the vacuum. That's what Nicholi used to call it. The once prosperous colony of over fifty thousand had been declining for the last decade. After settlement on the moon had opened up, people found lunar life more stable. It had been so gradual.

Charley was jarred awake as he instinctively grabbed the side of the ladder. His heart beat fast as he took several deep breaths. He almost passed out at a place where gravity could take part in his demise.

"Steady, old friend. You've lost a lot of blood, and you must keep your head clear. Look above, just a few meters to that ledge and we're almost there."

**"My other self, my counsel's consistory,
My oracle, my prophet, my dear cousin,
I, as a child, will go by thy direction."**

Fatigue overcame Charley as he reaching the narrow cat walk. Sitting and leaning against a wall felt good. A soft dim light filtered through a half-a-meter-square grill in front of him. People would be in there. The kind of souls that live in that realm of light and seeing, not hiding in fear. Charley knew that if he went into that world, they would look at him, and ask him questions, and hurt him.

"Please Nicholi, please don't make me go."

"You got to. If you stay here, you'll die. I know you're tired, but closing your eyes will mean you never wake up. The other side of that screen can't be worse then death. Come on, it's simple. Grab the grill and pull."

Charley lifted the wounded arm up with his good hand to get his fingers through the holes. He gave the panel a tug —it held. Lowering his head, his mind drifted.

"You call that an effort? Yank on that thing. Get some weight behind it. Forget the pain, pull harder. HARDER."

The panel gave way, Charley fell backwards. The bulky metal shifted to the side. He heard a crack and screamed out in pain. Carefully he removed his hand, hot shooting agony radiating from the left index finger. The digit pointed at an oblique angle from the rest. The broken bone shocked him to a fresh awareness.

On all fours he crept to the opening, to an environment of clean walls and carpeting. The bright hallway had no signs of people.

"Almost home, Charley-my-boy."

> **"Let us go in together,**
> **And still your fingers on your lips, I pray.**
> **The time is out of joint. O cursed spite**
> **That ever I was born to set it right!**
> **Nay, come, let's go together."**

Knees and elbows got him to a room that shined, and stung the nose with an antiseptic smell.

"Now, get up in that machine and Nicholi will do the rest."

He made his way to a large metal cabinet that dominated one wall. Dread of the strange room overcame him. The walls seemed to crowd in on his being. He turned, longing for the door and the darkness beyond.

"No, Charley, there's no use running."

"Leave me alone, Nicholi. Go away."

"I can't."

Charley hesitated. How could his friend be so cruel? How could he inflict this anguish on him? Painfully, he crawled onto the shelf set inside the huge mechanical apparatus.

"Autodoc model seven-fifty-D activated," a cold unemotional voice said from everywhere.

"Aye, my buddy Charley here needs to be fixed up."

"Which input mode do you request — manual, auto-physical, auto-extended-physical-physiological?" asked the voice.

"Extended. Give us the works. Charley deserves the best."

**"The miserable have no other medicine
But only hope:
I have hope to live, and am prepared to die."**

"Nicholi, don't go. Get me out of here," Charley shouted. Fear flooded his mind as he heard new sounds from the machine. There were small movements inside the shelf where he lay. Pieces of his ripped clothing were moved. He felt changes made to his body as cold metal claws touch and scratched. His frightened screams faded as he slipped into unconsciousness.

* * *

Charley opened his eyes, to see an attractive middle-aged woman with short dark hair looking down at him. Lying on his back in a dimly-lit room, he felt tied up. He realized he was confined by bandages and the sheet covering him.

"Mr. Charles Tailor, I presume. My name is Marta Sheldon. I'm a Med-tech here at the Medical Center. Last night we found a trail of blood leading to you from the hallway. It took a great deal of courage for you to get here. You are very fortunate. Another half hour and you would have been dead. But, of course, you're lucky we were here at all. It's hardly worth keeping a medical team. Except for the small retirement community, and service personnel. That and a few dozen Scavengers who keep running away and hiding from us."

"You're responding well to all the treatments, but you need lots of rest," she said, looking over the reports on the screens. Returning her attention to him, she smiled. "You even cleaned up pretty well."

"Where's Nicholi? He helped me."

"He's not here. You get some rest, and we'll talk about it later," she said with a reassuring voice and turned to leave.

"No. We must find him. He saved my life." Charley sat up in bed, finding it a painful position. He feared for Nicholi, and needed to talk to him.

"Mr. Tailor, the Autodoc was set to address physiological problems, as well as physical. You were suffering from multiple personality schizophrenia." She looked back to the records. "Nicholi was one of your other personalities."

"No, he isn't. He's real." Charley reached out, grabbing the doctor's arm.

"Nicholi, Toby, Sergeant Hector, Sir. Anthony, the actor. You've had a lot of guests in there. The Autodoc took preliminary steps to correct the problem. We have more work to do in this area, and you'll be meeting with specialists to continue treatment."

Somehow he knew she was right. Whatever the machine had done, it made him aware of the truth. "Nicholi was my friend, and I'll miss him."

She gently eased him back down, and carefully placed his arm at his side.

"Don't be sad, Mr. Tailor," she said, smiling. "We should always be our own best friend. And besides," she put her hand on his chest over his heart, and gently gave him a pat, "I think Nicholi is right here."

END

AUTHORS COMMENTS

My hat is off to Shakespeare.

I love the idea of large habitats in space, although, I'm not sure why you would leave the ground or the moon to live there. For a writer it was a fun place to play.

I hope that we can all learn to be our own best friends.

HAMPERED

Roger froze. The razor, mid-stroke, hung motionlessly next to his face. His shaving cream reflection in the mirror searched for anything behind him. He had definitely heard a sound, deep and menacing enough to shake the sturdiest of legs. The small studio apartment couldn't hide anything big enough to make that noise.

He cautiously walked past his closet and looked around his small living space. Every scattered dirty sock, half-used glass, empty chip bag, and newspaper remained just as he left it.

"I said, excuse me," came a booming voice from the other end of the room.

Roger flung himself forward onto the unmade foldout bed. His fright propelled him up the back to embrace the wall. He turned around and slid into the corner, sucking air as fast as his heartbeat. His head settled inches from the ceiling.

"Who said that?" Demanded, Roger. Every system in his body continued to race in the fight or flight condition.

"Will you calm down?" The rumbling voice replied. "It's only me."

"Yeah, but where are you? And who the hell are you?"

"Allow me to introduce myself. I'm PJ, your clothes hamper."

Roger focused past the clutter in the room, and onto the white woven basket at the end of the closet. The lid lay back, resting opened against the wall, and a T-shirt draped over the edge. His fear began to subside. How dangerous could a hamper be?

"Who's in there?" Roger said, looking down into the dark cavity that made up PJ.

"There's nobody else here. Just you and me kid. I'm sorry for the startling intro, but I couldn't think of a softer way of making myself known."

"That's all right," said Roger, continuing to examine the almost empty container. "Are you animated?"

"You mean can I like jump around and stuff? No. This is about it. And I'm glad you moved me out of the closet. The dark is depressing."

Roger lifted the T-shirt hanging on PJ's rim, and let it slide inside.

"Oh, yeah. Thank you. That's so good. You've been teasing me with that underwear for days."

"What are you talking about?"

"I get nourishment from dirty clothes. And let's face it, you leave them scattered all over the room. I'm about starving here."

"I get it," Roger pointing his finger at the basket, and backed away. "You're the one who eats my socks, and leaves me with odd pairs," he accused.

"No, no, that's not me. You should talk to the washer and dryer about the missing socks. I only feed off their odors. Your shorts after playing basketball on Saturday, is as tantalizing to me, as pizza is to you."

"This is amazing." Roger sat on the edge of the bed. "Wait until Jimmy and Frank see you. They're going to have a meltdown."

"No. I'm sorry. The standard rule of non disclosure applies. I can't reveal myself to anyone."

"But you did it to me. Why are you talking now?"

"I've decided to help you with your problems."

"I don't have problems." Roger went back to finish his shave. He knew he had lots of situations and he could use some help with, but not from his clothes hamper.

"Oh, I see. How long have you been out of work?"

"It's only been four months."

"I can help you."

"How?" Roger asked with a touch of sarcasm. "Are you some kind of magic hamper? Are you going to give me three wishes?"

"No. I can't do that. But I know clothes, and clothes make the man. And besides, what have you got to lose?"

PJ was right. Even thinking that was uneasy for Roger to accept. There had to be something enchanted about a talking clothes hamper. Maybe his luck had changed. He would give it a try.

"All right, PJ, what would you like me to do?"

"Your interview isn't until later this afternoon?"

"Yeah. How did you know about that?"

"Because I've been listening longer than I've been talking."

"Of course, the phone. Sorry."

"I want you to go to a good quality men's store, and get a few items. Then bring them back, and I'll put together an ensemble that will knock them out of their underwear. We'll start with a good Oxford shirt. Get some blues and stripes."

*　*　*

Roger burst into his apartment. Nothing could hold back his excitement.

"PJ, it worked."

"Did you get it?" A deep voice responded.

"No. Better then that."

"Well, kid, tell me before I have to yank it out of you."

"The Personnel Director liked me so much that he had me interview for a different job. A much better and higher paying job."

"Very good, kid. So how did it turn out?"

"I start Monday. I can't believe it. Thank you, PJ."

"It's all part of the service—fashion consulting, storage of soiled unmentionables, etc. There's no time to lose. We have to get started."

"What are you talking about? I got the job."

"Yeah, kid. But can you keep it? We need to work on your self image, presence, and confidence."

"Great. Just what I need, people skills from a clothes hamper."

"Then, of course, you'll have to clean your room."

* * *

"Here we are," Roger said, as he slowly opened the door.

"This isn't so bad," the young woman said.

"Well, it's pretty small." Roger pocketed his keys.

"I shared a room with two other girls in college, and it wasn't this big."

"Have a seat, Victoria. Would you like something to drink, a soda or a beer?" Roger joined her on the couch.

"No, thank you. I'm fine. You know, I've been wanting for you to ask me out, ever since you started working in our department." She tucked strands of chestnut hair behind her ear, and moved a little closer.

He leaned forward. "I noticed you right away, and was hoping you would go out with me."

A hideous noise startled them.

"What was that?" She squeaked.

"Nothing, it's just the TV."

"That sounded like T-Rex clearing its throat, and the TV is off. What's going on?"

Roger didn't have time to answer. The lid of the clothes hamper flew open. Dirty garments began to spew out in all directions. A deep rumbling growl rattled the dishes in the adjoining kitchenette. Her screams followed her all the way out of the apartment and down the hall.

"Wait. Come back. I can explain." Roger started to follow. But a blue double-knit put-over landed across his face. He couldn't see, and hit the door jam.

"What the hell was that all about?" Roger asked once he'd regained consciousness.

"I got sick at the way you were carrying on, and threw up," PJ answered.

"How could you? Victoria was the first girl I ever got to come to my apartment."

"That's not the kind you want to be dealing with."

"Are you kidding? She was pretty, and she liked me."

"I just can't abide them."

"What are you talking about?" Roger's voice turned cold.

"You know. They wear those frilly, little stringy things. And those sweet artificial odors are hard on my digestion."

Roger finally understood what had happened. Pulling off his shoe, he went out into the hall, smashed the glass on the big red box with his size ten, and grabbed the fire axe. Any Ninja executioner would have envied the firm grip Roger had on the handle as he lifted it over his head.

"Wait. I don't deserve this," PJ's voice pleaded.

"You're right," Roger said, slowly lowered the axe to his side. "You deserve worse."

* * *

The man in brown shorts with a tan to match plopped the box onto the scales. He then transferred information onto other form.

"Are you one of them?" He asked, with a grin, pointing to the address.

"No," Roger replied, rather embarrassed. "I'm mailing it for a friend."

"It's going to cost you. Florida is a long way," the man said. He tossed the package into the back of the brown van. A low rumbling moan escaped from the truck.

"What was that?"

"I didn't hear anything," Roger lied.

"So, you have friends at . . . ," the man glanced at the paperwork, "West Beach Nudist Community?"

"Not yet. But I will when this package arrives," Roger said, eagerly signing the receipt.

END

AUTHORS COMMENTS

Have you ever been in your bathroom participating in a number two and look at the clothes hamper for a long time?

A FAIRY'S TAIL

Eating lunch with a Fire-Lizard isn't as bad as you might think. Their manners aren't that different from ours, and better than most other species. We sat together because of the "getting-along-with-each-other" policy which our governments had set up.

Their real name is the Tri-Bah and it's not like they really breathed fire. No, that's just a myth. The name comes from their coloration. Their meter-and-a-half frame starts with thin muscular legs and the lower torso a deep rich brown. At mid-chest their body turns reddish, then into a pure red, and blending into orange and yellows at the shoulders. From the neck up, they are bright yellow. Except of course, they have the three black spots on their forehead. They are a living caricature of a burning stick or torch.

"Is it true," I asked my dining companion, Due'quok, "that the parents of Fire-Lizards have the spots on their children's forehead surgically altered at birth?"

"It is one of those things that is not talked about, but freely done. That portion of the body is covered until after the procedure." The electronic translator sitting on the table between us finally replied.

"Why is it so important?" I asked.

"Perfectly round, same-sized spots in a good pattern are a sign of breeding, nobility and strength."

"We do similar stuff like that, also."

Although cordial and corporative, Due'quok wasn't talkative. I had run out of questions to ask two days after this trade exchange started. You know, one of those sharing-technology-with-once-enemies-now-friends, kind of meeting.

During the quiet, I remembered one of the last things I did before coming to the conference. I told my seven-year-old daughter of my upcoming trip, and my nervousness in meeting these creatures. It is said that humans have a natural fear of reptiles. She didn't think so, and became restless. I decided to read her a story before bed, one of her favorites, <u>The Prince and His New Bicycle</u>. She had a question for the Fire-Lizards.

"So, Due'quok," I asked, "do you have any fairy tales in your culture?"

He glared at me with an intensity I had not seen before. His large pupils formed narrow vertical slits. The briefing I had on this species and my instincts told me this was not a good sign.

"How did you know about that?" he spat.

"I'm just curious. I meant no offense." I truly didn't. His teeth were bigger and sharper than mine. I had no idea what could have upset him so much.

He took a moment to compose himself before continuing.

"A young boy went with his family on a . . ." The translator revolted in a long string of noises at his input. After conversing with Due'quok, the machine continued. ". . . trip, slash, safari to reestablish links to family and the past."

"We might call that a vacation," I offered. The translators hadn't gotten our two languages totally worked out.

"They had set up camp," Due'quok continued, "at the foothills of the Old Teeth Mountains. All started well in this beautiful hunting range. But that evening the boy's clumsiness scared away dinner. His siblings took pleasure with many jabs and laughter, at his expense.

"During that night the boy sought to redeem himself. He would climb up to the mountains, and catch the legendary Golden Fairy of that region. The naive child didn't know that fairies were only mythological, and no evidence has ever been produced that they existed. There were reports of them quickly flying away from intruders. But they were merely streaks of light on recording equipment."

"So, it's hard to catch them?" I asked.

"Yes. But the boy had fools' luck. In the early morning mist he saw a Golden Fairy drinking moisture off the leaves of a tack-a-tu bush."

Due'quok's eyes became large and dilated. He stared at a point far behind me.

"The boy carefully approached the hovering light. The luminous wings blurred and reflected off the golden scales of its small body. The boy crept very close. With one swift movement, he grabbed the fairy.

The wingspan was about the size of a hand." Due'quok held up a spread open claw of his finger and two thumbs in front of me.

"The boy had to be watchful of the fairy's sharp teeth. A good bite and the child's finger might release his redemption."

"If you let me go, I will grant you a wish," the fairy said, bowing to the boy.

"My wish is to keep you with me, so that I may redeem myself, and prove to my family that I'm a good hunter," said the boy.

"I cannot grant you that wish. That would dishonor me and my people."

"And I cannot let you go for the same reason."

"We are at an impasse. And I can see that your honor is at stake as well. Therefore, we must part our ways," said the fairy.

Due'quok moved his gaze back to me. I looked into his large eyes. I had never seen one of these creatures so sad. I felt privileged to see this expression of emotion.

"The Golden Fairy turned tail and ran," he continued. "All the child saw was a luminous streak disappearing into the mist. He climbed back down the mountain to his family. His siblings rejoiced at his return, and pronounced him the greatest hunter."

"Wait a minute," I interrupted. "How did they know that he caught the Golden Fairy? He didn't bring him back to prove his story was true. Did they take him at his word, or what? The story needs more details in order for it to ring true."

"Do you not believe me?" Due'quok looked sad.

"That's not the point. I'm talking about for the sake of the story."

Due'quok reached into that pouch at his belt, identical to those worn by all the Fire-Lizards. He removed a small box, and opened it to show me its contents. Inside was a thin golden scaled ribbon, coiled and tapered to the tip.

"You see. I caught the fairy by its tail. Although he could not honor my wish, and stay my captive, he did leave enough behind to corroborate my story."

When I returned home and told my daughter of this wonderful adventure of Due'quok, she was delighted. She especially liked the idea of a reptilian race having lizard-like golden fairies. She begged me to write it down, to keep forever. And that is what I have done.

This just goes to show you that one man's story is another's fairy's tail.

END

AUTHORS COMMENTS

Have you ever caught a little garden lizard by its tail? It has always fascinated me how it will detach its tail and run away. How wonderful.

This story takes place after the story in a book I'm writing, *"Sorrow's Edge."* It has the Tri-Bah and humans and others involved in doing, what I hope people will find as, interesting things.

THE CORNER OF
SESAME AND ELM

M ajor Jacobs paused outside the door of
the room. He tried to calm his nerves and
settle his stomach. This was his first time beyond
the warning signs and security. The Senator waited
inside, and wouldn't be alone. Yet there would be the
glass partition — one inch thick, built proof, shatter
resistant. He should be safe.

Reaching for the large cold metal handle that
sealed off the area, he hesitated, his mind flooding
with all the rumors and gossip. Were the stories true?
His training hadn't prepared him for a confrontation
beyond the scope of any war, cold or hot in this world

of the late 1950's. He swallowed hard, and opened the passage to an unbelievable reality.

Only two wooden chairs sat on one side of the glass wall, and on the other stood the aliens. The Senator didn't greet him. Both stared at the incredible monsters looking back at them.

One had purple fur, large white eyes, yellow fangs, and a green nose. His companion was different, with reddish matted fur, small black eyes, no nose, and yellow feathers on its feet. Their arms were almost useless on bloated bodies, and appeared to waddle even when not walking.

Major Jacobs could not understand how such grotesque creatures existed. His skin crawled and the hair on the back of his neck stood up. Nausea and fear set his heart racing and his intestines churning.

"Please continue," The Senator said.

"When we return, in forty of your years," rumbled the deep raspy voice of the beast with large eyes, "all your questions shall be answered. You will be given the knowledge to travel the stars, cure your diseases, and provide every comfort for all your people. We're unequipped to do that now. We are but humble scouts, looking for other superior intelligent life with whom we may find fellowship."

"That is very encouraging," The Senator said. "We look forward to the arrival of your ambassador in forty years, and we will not tell anyone that you were here."

"You must not tell. It is important that you understand what we have learned from the past. A species knowing of impending prosperity will turn lazy and corrupt before we arrive. We do not wish this on you and your people."

"That makes sense," the Senator replied as he stood up to leave. "Have a safe journey." The Senator motioned to Major Jacobs, and they left.

*   *   *

"Did you taste it?" the feather-footed creature asked after the humans left. "The sweet pungent flavor of fear running down your throat."

"It was good and nourishing. I feel stronger and more refreshed than I have felt in a long time. The terror from these animals is easy to harvest, and our kind will gorge on them for a millennium."

"Yes, we shall drink deep of the horror when we bring the others to feast."

* * *

Major Jacobs followed the Senator down a long hall and they entered a small office near the front of the large wooden hangar. He removed his glasses and rubbed the bridge of his nose. Dry desert winds picked up outside, and in his uniform he felt uncomfortably warm. They sat down at an old table amid dusty furnishings unused since World War II.

"That was draining," the Major said.

"Yes, I felt it myself," the Senator replied. "I wanted you to see firsthand what we are dealing with, so you can better handle your next job."

"Just what is my assignment?" The Major knew his presence was requested for a reason, but he didn't understand what.

"I'm going to keep a lid on this. We can deny this ever happened and keep the public misguided, side-tracked, and confused until <u>they</u> come back. That won't be difficult. But, we must do something to get our people ready to deal with their return. That's where you come in."

"I'm not sure I follow, sir."

"You saw <u>them</u>. We have to get everyone ready for the encounter with those creatures, protecting ourselves from panic, and doing it without the world knowing. Those are our first concerns. That is your assignment. With your experience in public relations, you come highly recommended. If there is anything you need, you'll get it."

* * *

"You're not the cartoonist?" the newly promoted Lieutenant Colonel Jacobs asked.

"No, I do puppets," the odd young man with a beard replied apologetically.

The whole incident in the desert seemed far away and very long ago. For over two years, Colonel Jacobs had not worn a uniform. Even his sandy hair grew to a length he could comb. The new lifestyle was just one outward sign of overall change.

Every aspect of his operation took so long. He now occupied an office on the eighteenth floor of a downtown business building — an event that required six months of scheming to acquire in an unsuspicious manner. All his activities must look like a normal civilian operation. The constant delays and covering up paperwork trails were getting on his nerves.

"Ah yes, here it is," he said, finding the right folder. "Mr. Hanley, I saw a performance you did last week. It was very unusual. If I remember correctly, you had this dog eating a mouse?"

"No, that was a bear, and he ends up eating a frog," Mr. Hanley corrected. "You must understand, that was just the punch line. The humor of my work doesn't lie in animals devouring each other."

"I thought it was very funny," Colonel Jacobs replied disarmingly. Removing a key from his pocket he unlocking the top drawer of his desk and took out a plain folder.

Mr. Hanley continued to defend his art form. "You see, I have been working on a group of barnyard puppets for children. I call them CRUMPETS, after the English cookie. They're easily recognized, and associated with kids. You see the word CRUMPET sort of rhymes with puppet. I'm hoping that eventually these CRUMPETS can teach in some manner."

"Mr. Hanley, I know what a crumpet is. I think you're doing some fine work. That's why I've asked you here. I believe we can help you get a good start." Colonel Jacobs said and removed a sheet of paper from the folder. He held it up for Mr. Hanley to see. "If you could make your puppets look like these, we could help you in many ways."

Colonel Jacobs watched the man's face, studying the pencil sketches of a monster with large eyes and one with feathery feet. The wheels were turning all right. Mr. Hanley's eyes grew intense and then widened.

"Those are very strange creatures." Then after a pause, "You were talking about some kind of aid?"

"The information I've got says you work alone in your apartment." Colonel Jacobs slipped the picture back into the folder, then into the desk. "How would you like a studio, and two assistants to help with construction of the puppets?"

A smile widened on the man's face.

Colonel Jacobs locked the drawer and put the key in his pocket.

Mr. Hanley repositioned himself in the chair. His face turned grim. "Why do you want me to create and use monsters? How can we entertain kids with something like this?"

"You know, Mr. Hanley," Colonel Jacobs rose, walked around, and sat on the corner of his desk, "if this works out as well as I think, we may get you a spot on the Ed Sullivan Show."

The young Mr. Hanley eagerly shook his hand, displaying an even bigger grin.

"Go on, and get your creative juices flowing. Next week we'll work out the details."

As Mr. Hanley closed the door behind him, Colonel Jacobs pushed the button on the intercom. "Terry, has that cartoonist shown up yet, or the guy who wants to make slasher movies?"

"No." Came the reply.

Colonel Jacobs tried to relax by looking out the window at the city. The ignorant swarms of humanity were unaware of what was to come. So much work had to be done.

Even if that puppet guy he just met caught on and did everything right, it would take years to make an impact. It would take much longer to establish a following and distribute the idea globally. The worst part was, no one could know what he was doing.

* * *

The retired Colonel Jacobs leaned back in his easy chair. His four-year-old granddaughter squirmed in his lap as they watched early morning TV. Thanks to the promises made so long ago, he had great hopes for his descendants. The time was close at hand for the return. Most of his life he feared that he would not live to see the affects of his work. Now, he was afraid he would see it. Age hardens the attitudes and he remembered too well the desert hangar filled with fear. Well, he had done what he could.

His granddaughter repeated the letters of the alphabet as a colorful orange furry creature with a big nose said them to the television audience. He hoped his efforts would be enough.

* * *

In a deserted portion of the park the spacecraft landed. Three hideous beasts emerged and made their way to a row of hedges that blocked them from view. One had purple fur and large white eyes. Another had reddish fur and yellow feathers on its feet. A blue one with long arms and an elephant-like nose led the way.

"The trip here has been long, and our kind are famished. Your report of this garden had better be true. The horde is waiting for the signal to land," the blue alien said, parting the shrubbery.

"Look, young animals. This is fortunate, for we believe they are easy to harvest. Come, this will make a grand meal," the red one said.

They forced their way through openings in the greenery and stood before a street corner. A large yellow vehicle was loading a vast quantity of small children from a brown structure.

A cherub-faced boy wearing a back pack and a red jacket spotted them first. His teachers knew about his excitable nature, but this went beyond even his most unpredictable mischief.

"CRUMPETS," he shouted, pointing to the three approaching beings. Every child turned to look. Eyes went wide in amazement as they shouted and squealed with glee. En masse they stormed across the boulevard.

The feast of sweet fear did not come. Instead it was sour. It dripped as bile acid into empty stomachs. The ingested was not palatable, but instead the festering remains of contaminated filth. Doing what only they could do, the children's complete and unquestioning love slashed ulcerated wounds in the intestines of the fleeing monsters.

The aliens retreated as fast as they could with tummy aches.

"This is a retched place you've brought us to. You will be punished for this blunder," said the blue one.

"We did not know," the other two pleaded.

They hobbled onto their spacecraft still holding their sides. They would never ever return to this spoiled junk food again.

END

AUTHORS COMMENTS

My mother gave me the idea for this story. We were looking at those brightly colored puppets on TV with my daughter. You know the ones, big noses and teaching children the alphabet.

"Their getting us ready for when the aliens land and take over," my mother said.

She was funny like that.

DANCE OF THE
SHEPHERDING
MOONS

I finished zipping up my space suit, and adjusted the settings on the control box at my side. It really isn't a space suit. That's what I called it. I sewed low voltage heating pads to the insides of an old pair of sweats. Even found a pair of electric socks and gloves. The only thing that keeps my face warm is my thick curly mustache. All the cables running back to the power supply were isolated, insulated and trip faulted to the point that I would never get shocked.

"What will we have for tonight Copernicus?" I said, scratching the ears of my black and white cat curled up on the plain, wooden bench. "How about some _Boney Ratte_?" Opening the cases, I loaded the CD player with the silvery discs. "And to get a head start on the holidays lets play _The Trans-Siberian Orchestra_. I know, We should start it all off with some _Guns and Roses_. That'll get us in the mood."

Copernicus said nothing. This is not unusual. He is a very quiet cat.

I cued up the CD, and hit the big red button on the wall behind the bench. The room was filled with the wine of motors moving something heavy.

Slowly turning around, I looked up, and allowed Slash's opening guitar riff of _Sweet Child of Mine_ to fill my soul. The parting roof exposed us to a brilliant display of stars piercing the inky sky. The patches of exposed skin on my face tingled as freezing desert air rushed in and slapped my face like a jealous woman.

Turning attentions to my logbook, I found the right page. Twisting the knob at the base of the telescope, it began to move. Another adjustment tilted it upwards.

"Sweet child of mine," I said, "let's see what we can see."

The familiar excitement settled in. I had been waiting for this all day. We had a cold clear night, Stirring music, honking in the background and my telescope. Every thing was in place.

"Wait a minute. Who's honking?"

Copernicus looked up, but was otherwise unresponsive.

Pulling the remote out of my side pocket, I muted the stereo. The observatory was built over my garage and the pointed roof slid back on rails to expose the telescope to the sky. There is a three foot high wall on the two opposite sides with the rails to keep people from walking off the roof.

I went to the edge and looked down. A Sheriffs' patrol car had parked in front of my house. The officer stood outside the vehicle waving at me.

"Is that you, Hans?" I yelled down.

"Yes, Ben. I tried the door bell, but it didn't work."

"I've been meaning to fix that."

"I hope I'm not disturbing you?"

"Just a little. What can I do for you on this gorgeous night?"

"The sheriff sent me to get you. He needs your help."

I didn't like the sound of that. Usually there were too many strings attached to those people. "If this is official business, he knows that I don't do that any more." I retired from the L.A.P.D. four years ago. This was not long after my friend, now Sheriff, Gary Richards moved out to the desert. I came out here a year later.

"Yes. He said you would say that. And I'm to bring you anyway."

"But its Thanksgiving."

"That's part of the problem."

"What if I refuse?"

"He said I could arrest you."

"In that case . . . give me a few minutes to change." I really didn't want to close up the observatory, but Gary wouldn't have taken such drastic measures if it wasn't important. "This had better be good," I said, as I carried Copernicus downstairs.

I lowered myself onto the front bench seat patrol car, and we sped off. The over worked sedan bumped and rocked as it went down the dirt road of Starlight Mesa Drive.

"Okay you got me in the car, what's going on?"

"There has been a murder on the other side of the valley, and the sheriff is involved. It took place at his uncle's house and he was there."

I easily switched to an old familiar professional state of mind that had been so comfortable many years ago. "What were they doing?"

"They were all having dinner with the rest of the family."

"Are you saying he's a suspect?"

"I'm sure he didn't do it. But he must be professional and not be a part of the investigation. So he asked me to get you to be an impartial adviser."

"That's crazy. Why can't Norman do it?" Paul Norman had been Yucca Valley's only detective for the last five years.

"He is occupied with a murder at a bar outside of Twenty Nine Palms, and there is also a knifing at the bowling alley."

"Busy night."

"You got that right. The sheriff said that he trusted you more than anyone else to be honest and objective."

"He must be desperate."

"You could say that," Hans turned onto Old Woman Springs Road. The hard pavement felt better with the over used springs of the patrol car.

"Tell me about the murder. Who is the victim?"

"That would be the Sheriff's uncle, David Tunny. He and his brother Harvey, and both their families had Thanksgiving dinner at the victim's home. The exceptions are the Sheriff's mother and the victim's daughter. Do you want me to tell you about the suspects?"

"Was there a weapon found?"

"A fork."

"What?"

"You know. One of those fancy carving set forks."

"Ouch. There should be prints on the handle."

"Sorry. The handle is smeared with gravy."

"Giblet?"

"I don't know. Is it important?"

"No. I'm just getting hungry. All right, tell me who the players are."

"First, there is the victim, David Tunny and his wife Margery. They have a daughter who is off at school. She has already been notified. There is the victims' brother, Harvey and his wife Katherine. They have two kids, Eve and Toby. Eve and her husband Bill Marks have three small children Sara, Tim and Nancy. The victim and his brother have a sister. She's Sheriff Richardson's mother and is back East visiting friends."

The road wound its way through the Mesa, and then started descending to the valley floor. The steep twists and turns gave way to a dazzling vista, a mirror of the sky. At least that's how I liked to think of a city at night. The uncountable tiny lights spread out over a large flat plain.

As beautiful as some people think this is astronomers have a special loathing for all cities at night. The one thing they can't stand is the light pollution making it hard to see the stars.

We crossed the 29 Palms Highway onto Joshua Lane and up a gentle rise to the other side of the Valley. Diverse housing is peppered throughout Yucca Valley, from little more that a shack to very modern upscale homes. We stopped at a home that met the latter description, a single story ranch style.

We got out of the car and saw Gary waiting outside. "What's going on Gary?" I asked.

"I'm so glad you're here, Ben. I'm not sure what I was going to do," he said, shaking his head back and forth.

"I haven't seen you this emotionally undone since we worked at the Rampart division," I said. At the time we were both rookies and not ready for the stark realities of being a cop as we thought. That had been a long time ago. "I'm not sure how I can help."

"The Coroner wants to move the body. Since Norman isn't here I had Joe go over the room. Maybe you could look at what he found and make sure he didn't miss anything. And we'll make sure that you get covered for your time."

"Don't worry Gary. You take it easy. I'm sure we can clear you of this whole thing."

"I'm not worried about that. I know I'm innocent. I just can't believe that one of my family members is capable of murder." His face carried a pain he couldn't hide.

Even though Gary should know better, is anyone ready to think of a member of their family capable of homicide? Yet everyone who commits such acts had a family. The human race is so naive. That's why I gave up law enforcement for the stars. The universe is anything but emotional, irrational, or stupid. It just IS in all its beauty.

I made my way into the house. The family all sat around the living room. A woman was crying, others looked sad, and the children were behaving like kids. I wasn't ready to talk to them yet. Hans directed me thru a door.

In a large family room off the kitchen at the back of the house, a long table set with the remains of all the thanksgiving fix'ns.

"It looks like the victim had a great last meal."

"Hi Ben," said Sheriff's Deputy Joe Rodriguez. "They said you were going to be here."

"Gary insisted. Well Joe, It looks like you have everything under control. I hope I'm not intruding." The last thing I wanted to do is to make these guys feel like I was sticking my nose in, or taking over. I would prefer to waste my time looking for dark matter in the crab nebula.

"Of course not. I would appreciate any pointers you could give me. I have helped out on these, a couple of times, but never on my own," said Joe, as he continued to write on his clipboard. The body lay back in a brown padded chair.

I got closer to examine the wound. "It appears the forks went between the ribs. It probably pierced the heart. I doubt if it would have been fatal otherwise."

"That's what I thought," said Joe. "But the autopsy will tell us for sure. The angle looks like the thrust was upwards, from below. Also, with his arms outward and the funny position of the one leg, I think maybe he was standing up, and then collapsed into the chair after being stabbed."

"Joe, I think you're onto something. Why don't you show me everything else you found?"

"Well, there's not much. You might have noticed there are four ways in or out. The door to the back leads to the patio and back yard, the one in the front leads to the kitchen, the one on that side goes to a hallway," Joe pointed his finger, "and the other to the porch."

"That porch goes around most of the house, doesn't it?"

"Yes."

I reviewed what little evidence Joe had found. One of the problems had to do with so many people being in the house. And of course they were all family.

"Are you guys done with the body?" The coroner asked as she came up to Joe and me.

Joe turned to me. "I think so," I said.

She finished up her job and removed the body. That left us alone.

"Who found the guy?" I asked.

"That would be Eve Marks, the victim's niece."

"I'm ready to ask a few questions. How about you, Joe?"

"Yeah, I'm ready. I'll have her come in." Joe turned for the door.

"I wonder if there is any pie left," I asked, unaware I said it out loud.

"No. I already asked."

"Too bad, the leftovers looked good." I was disappointed.

A man and a woman in their late twenties entered the room. He held her hand in an obvious gesture of support. She had been crying and her makeup looked terrible.

"Hi," I said. "My name is Ben and I'm sorry about your grief. But I need to ask you a few questions relating to when you found your Uncle." I reached out and gave each of them a polite hand shake and looked them straight in the eye. I wanted their reaction to this room, to the situation and to my authority. I will repeat this ritual with every suspect.

"I'm Bill and this is my wife Eve. I hope you don't mind if I join you while you question her? She's still a little shook up."

"No, not at all. It will save me the trouble of talking with you later." Normally, I wouldn't allow it. But this is a small town, and we could always separate them later if I had some tougher questions. Eve's eyes kept darting to the chair where the victim had been and then quickly looking away. "So, tell me what happened."

"I was in the kitchen helping with the clean up. I thought I would come out here and gather some plates." She hesitated. "That's when I found him in the chair. At first I thought he might have been asleep, lying back in the chair. But then I saw the fork sticking out of him, and the blood."

"What did you do?" I asked, wanting to keep the story flowing.

"I'm not sure what I did after that. I think I screamed."

"You did." Her husband said, "We all heard you."

"Then everyone came in. And I don't remember a lot after that. You must understand that not only did I love my uncle, but he looks just like my father. They were twins, you know."

"Did you happen to touch the body?"

"I guess so. I shook his arm to wake him up. Then I screamed." She said.

"How was your relationship with your uncle?" I asked this to both of them.

"It was fine. He was a nice man and loved our children." She seemed earnest.

"How about you, Mr. Marks?"

"We got along fine."

"I want you to tell me anything you heard," I turned my attention back the Ms. Marks. "Anyone you might have seen, or anything odd you sensed?"

"Not much," she said. "You could hear voices from the living room, and the children had the TV on in the bedroom. But nothing else."

"How about you, Mr. Marks? Where were you before your wife screamed?"

"I was in the living room talking to my father-in-law."

"How long were you there?"

"We were having a long discussion about the new venture."

"Explain to me what that means."

"Sure," he said, shifting his stance. "You see every few years the family sells the business and starts another. They have been doing that for as long as they've been old enough to buy anything."

"What is the new business?"

"They hadn't settled on anything yet. But I did hear them talking about something in the automotive industry."

"How much money is involved?"

"Not a lot; just our livelihood. So, some of us weren't happy with the idea of changing now. We though that everything was going very good as it is."

"I see. Tell me, Mr. Marks, what business is the family in now?"

"A bakery. We have two stores and provide most of the restaurants in the Morongo basin."

"Excuse me officer," Eve interrupted. "Are you done with me? I would really like to go sit down." She looked pale. "And I have to look in on Sara."

"That's our three-year-old daughter," Bill added.

"Sure Ms. Marks. You may go."

"I think the fact that he looked so much like her father has had a deeper impact then she realizes," her husband said, as she stepped into the other room.

"Mr. Marks, who was missing from the room before your wife screamed?"

"Let me think." He lowered his glance and lines of concentration appeared on his forehead. "Toby wasn't there. I think he went out for a smoke. And Katherine was gone. No, she went in with the rest of us. She must have been there. And of course, Eve and Margery were in the kitchen."

"And Margery is?"

"The victim's wife," answered Joe.

"Thank you, Mr. Marks."

I rolled around the names in my mind that came up in the conversation. It was a good selection. "Who should be next?"

"Let's talk to Toby," said Joe.

"Good choice."

Joe smiled as he went to retrieve the next suspect.

Toby wore short hair and stubbly beard so popular at the time, t-shirt, baggy shorts, and an attitude completed his ensemble.

"Hello Mr. Tunny," I said, sticking out my hand. "You're Eve Mark's brother?"

"Yeah."

"What were you doing before your uncle's body was found?"

"Ripping a Juul."

"What?"

"Having a vape."

"Ho. Where?"

"On the porch."

"Can you be a little more specific?"

"You know. I sat for a while. I walked back and forth for a while. Then I strolled out to the driveway, looked up at the stars, and did a pirouette before coming back in." Toby's gestures were as mocking as his words.

"This isn't funny," said Joe.

I found myself with a flash of envy. If this jerk got to look at the stars, then why couldn't I? I told myself to regain concentration and rubbed my eyes.

"Tell me Mr. Tunny, where do you work?"

"At the family business. We all do."

"How did you feel about this new business?"

"The new 'venture,' as they like to call it, is a joke. There is nothing wrong with the one we have. It's doing well. In fact, it's growing. Things couldn't be better. And they want to dump it."

"Could you please tell me about your job?"

"Who are you, anyway? You're not a cop," he said with a strange look on his face.

"He may not be, but I am." Joe moved a little closer.

"You're right. I'm an independent contractor retained by the San Bernardino County Sheriffs Department to help facilitate this investigation and insure due process integrity over the reach of this jurisdiction," I said as pleasantly as I could. Sometimes a little techno-babble can change the direction of the questioning. Once a suspect took a punch at me, but most of the time it got things started again. This guy just smiled.

"We own a bakery. That may not sound like much, especially out here."

"What do you do, specifically?"

"I do all the deliveries to the restaurants. I have two guys that work for me. And we make the rounds every morning."

"I take it you were happy with this arrangement?"

"Yes. I haven't done too well in the past, you know, finding my niche in the world. This is the best job I ever had. Not to mention all the really nice waitress I've met."

"Other than your disagreement with your uncle over the business, how was your relationship with him?"

"He was a jerk." Toby's expression never changed.

"Did you kill him?" I asked, very carefully.

"No. I was going to quit the family and keep my job with the new owners of the bakery," he said, with a defiant smile.

"Mr. Tunny, which of these three doors did you use this evening?"

"I don't remember."

"While you were outside, whom else did you see or hear?"

"No one. I did heard my sister scream. That's all. Yeah, now I do remember. That's the way I went out," he said, pointing to the porch entrance.

"And how did you get back in?" I asked.

"Front door."

"I see. When you came in was anybody missing?"

"Aaaa."

I think he was trying to look inside his mind. At least that's what he looked like.

"Ya, the guys on the drive way weren't there. They and every one in the living room had gone into the family room." He stopped talking.

"Thank you, Mr. Tunny. Please wait in the living room. We may need you again."

"Whatever."

I went over to the side door and looked at it closely. "Did anyone check these doorknobs for prints?"

"Yes. All we got were smudges," said Joe.

"All right, who's our next contestant," I said, gesturing like a game show host. I was getting a little impatient. If it keeps going at this rate, we won't be done until sunrise.

"I think we should talk to Katherine Tunny, the brother's wife," Joe said. "Bill Marks couldn't remember if she was in the room or not."

"Sounds like a good idea. Send her in."

She wore a sad hollowed look on her face. Her hands had rung the life out of a paper napkin. The emotional toll was obvious.

"Hello my name is Ben," I said, sticking out my hand.

"Why are you men still here?" She asked, gently taking my hand.

"We're trying to gather evidence to find out who killed your husband's brother."

"But why here? Shouldn't you be combing the hills or setting up road blocks?"

"There has been nothing to suggest that the murderer was from outside the family. Unless you have some insight, we don't know about. Whom did you see? Anything unusual or odd?"

"No one."

"Nobody has seen anything," I said.

"Are you saying that one of us did this terrible thing?" She asked gripping the napkin.

"Yes I am."

"I don't see how that could be. A family member?"

"It happens." I wished they could understand just how common it was for family involvement.

"How was your relationship with Dave?" I asked.

"Katherine and I are the best of friends. Dave and I don't have a lot to say to each other." She said, ringing the napkin one more time.

THE CURSE OF TECUMSEH: AND OTHER STORIES

"Now, Ms. Tunny, where were you when Eve Marks screamed?"

"She's my daughter, you know." The sadness lingered. "I was sitting in the living room."

"How long had you been there?"

"I had been sitting for a while, but most of the time after dinner."

"That implies that you went somewhere."

"I went to the bathroom."

"That's a great idea," I said, a little more energetic than I expected. The two gave me an odd look. "Joe, could you please stay with Ms. Tunny for a little while?"

"Sure."

"Where was that bathroom again?"

"Thru there, on your right," she said, pointing to the side door.

"Thank you." I carefully let myself into a darkened hallway. A dim night light from the bathroom gave out an inviting golden glow. The neatness and decoration made it clear that this room was for guests. I washed the smell of giblets off my hands using a small carved pink soap. I wondered how Gary was holding up. I dried my hands on a tiny ornate towel. I was thinking it may be time to check in on him.

At the end of the hall and to the right it entered into the living room. Gary wasn't there, but Hans pointed to the outside. I found him on the driveway, leaning on his pickup and talking to someone looking like the victim.

"Hi, Ben, how is it going?" asked Gary.

"All right."

"I would like you to meet my uncle Harvey. I've been telling him about you." We shook hands.

"I'm sorry," I said, "that we had to meet under these circumstances."

"Of course. I understand that you and Gary have worked together for many years in L. A. before he moved out here."

"That's right. In fact he is the one who got me hooked on the high desert. I'm an amateur astronomer and this sky up here is incredible."

"Yes. I suppose it is."

"I wonder if I might ask you a few questions?" I couldn't pass up the opportunity to question the victim's brother.

"Of course not."

"I understand that some of the family isn't happy about the new business."

"They'll get over it."

"Are you sure?"

"Yes. And what does that have to do with anything?"

"It may be the motive. Tell me why someone would be more upset with your brother than with you about the new business."

"I don't see why anyone would be upset. This is nothing new. Everybody knows our intentions. We have done this before and we will do it again. It was our unique business plan. And they will do their part, because they are family."

"So you're saying you would receive the same hostility that your brother got?" I had just got an insight into the relative's frustration.

"Yes. Although, it is his turn."

"What do you mean by that?"

"He gets to choose the type of business. I chose the bakery last time, and wrote up that business plan. Now it was to be his turn. He was thinking about an auto parts store." He became saddened.

I realized that he had just started to speak of his brother in the past tense. The loss was sinking in.

"Will you excuse me for a moment?" He said, turning for the house.

"You know, Gary, this whole situation reminds me of twin moons around Saturn," I said, thinking of things much more fun to do. "They are called Shepherding moons. One is orbiting in a slightly lower orbit than the other. And the remains of a shattered moon lay between them, making up one of the smaller rings. They're called the shepherding because the gravitational field between them keeps the small ring, or in this case the family, in line."

"Why are you telling me this?" Gary interrupted. "Shouldn't you be trying to figure out who killed my uncle?"

"Oh, I'm doing that."

"You are? I told you, I didn't do it."

"Yes, Gary, I know. I've known you long enough to understand you could never do this. The idea of you killing someone is just not in your nature."

"I'm glad you think so."

"Let's go back inside, okay. As I was saying," I continued, as we walked back to the house. "Because the moon in the lower orbit travels faster than the other, there will be a time when it will try to pass the slower one. When this happens the two moons do this little dance as they pull on each other and swing themselves around. In the process, they exchange places. The one in the lower faster orbit is now in the upper slower one, and vice versa."

I found myself back in the large room with Joe and the victim's sister-in-law. Gary's serious expression made it obvious that he didn't care about the moons of any planet.

"Come on Ben, let's get on with it. Whom do you need to talk with?"

"Right now I need to talk with Joe for a moment," I said, motioning Joe to a corner of the room. "While I was gone, how was Ms Tunny?"

"About the same. She looked all depressed and moody. She also wanted to sit down and I let her."

"How did she treat that napkin she's holding?"

"That thing is about dead. She's been working on it nonstop," said Joe, as he gave me a squinty-eyed glance.

"Let's get this over with, Joe."

"Okay Gary," I tried to smile. Then I remembered the personal involvement of the Sheriff. "Ms Tunny," We turned and looked at her. She stood up as I continued, "Please tell us what happened the last time you were in this room."

She put her hand over her mouth as if trying to hide the shock on her face. "What are you talking about?"

"You know what I'm talking about. People didn't see you in the living room."

"I told you. I went to the bathroom," she said, looking even more strained.

"Then why are your hands sticky and you still have that napkin?" I hated saying that, but I always disliked this part of my old job. "You went to the bathroom, washed your hands, and then came out here and picked up the greasy serving fork."

"No!" She quickly looked at all of us with pain on her face. "I didn't mean to. I was upset. He could be more stubborn than my husband. I need to sit down."

Joe moved a chair from the dining table and steadied it behind her. She almost collapsed into it. She looked down at her hands and the wad of a napkin.

"Tell us what happened," I asked in a soft low voice.

"I Thought I would help clear the table. And David was in here."

"How did you get in here?"

"That way." She pointed to the side hall door. "I had just used the restroom."

"Go on, Ms. Tunny, what happened next?"

"We started talking. I told him that there was a way so that everyone could be happy with the new venture. All he had to do was to pick a bakery again as the next business. That way he could have his turn and the kids would be happy because they could keep what they have worked so hard for." She began to struggle with her words. "He just laughed and told me to stay out of it. That he and Harvey were making it happen. I called him an arrogant fool."

Again it became difficult for her.

"Please continue."

"He then called me names. Terrible names. I was infuriated and lunged out at him." She looked up and her sad eyes darted from one to another. "I didn't even remember having something in my hands. He gasped, and fell backwards into the chair. I couldn't believe what I had done. All I could do was run out of the room."

"You grabbed a napkin off the table before you left, didn't you?"

She looked down and slowly opened her hands. "I guess I did."

I looked at Gary and waited for recognition.

The Sheriff nodded his head. "Joe, would you please take Ms. Tunny into custody," he said in a polite voice.

*   *   *

I got into Hans' patrol car. The Sheriff bent over to talk thru the window.

"Why don't you come by the office tomorrow afternoon and we can finish things up?"

"Sure."

"Okay, Ben, how did you know it was Katherine?"

"I shook her hand. And it was still a little sticky from the gravy."

"How did you know it was gravy?"

"It smelled like giblets."

"Go on home, and look at your stars," Gary said, sarcastically waving the car on.

I decided to change the agenda for the night's observation. The crab nebula could wait. Maybe I should give Saturn another look. It had taken on a special relevance.

"Say, Hans, has anyone ever told you about the dance of the Shepherding Moons?"

END

AUTHORS COMMENTS

I liked writing about Yucca Valley. My dad and mom homesteaded out at Landers, not far from there. I've spent many a-day, looking for road runners, listening to the wind and watching the sun set. And of course the stars are spectacular.

I may have to do more writing using that location.

A special thanks to Scotty for his insight.

EARNING HIS WINGS

Melissa walked through the front door of her condo, and headed for the bedroom. She ignored the large mess of scattered clothes all over the bed and floor. Being a tidy person, she knew it had happened again. She went straight to the shelf above the far night stand.

It couldn't be the baby sitter making the mess. She didn't have a baby. The maid was also out of the question. She didn't have one of those either. No, her money stays bet on the weird guy at the end of the hall.

She fumbled with the camcorder she had set up to record the room while she was gone. Opening the little screen, she pushed the buttons to play back the video. Those shows were all over the TV. The shocking videos of what the sick-o's do in your home while you're gone. Well, this pervert would pay for his jollies. Film at eleven.

With the video beginning, Melissa fast forwarded until she found some action. It didn't take long. It must have happened right after she left for her morning run. But something wasn't right. She started it a second time, and put it on slow-mo. Her heart began to race as she watched in disbelief. She played it a few more times, but the images made less sense.

She stood there in terror at the realization of the presence of another entity. She carefully put down the camcorder, and slowly moved to the closet opposite the bed.

Her hands shook worse then after a 10K run. Cautiously, she opened the door, and removed the Number One Supper Mono Titanium driver from her golf bag. As she walked toward the bathroom, she brought the club over her right shoulder. But just before she could swing . . .

"Don't hurt me," a loud rumbling voice pleaded.

Melissa screamed, dropped the weapon, and ran back to the closet.

"What are you?" She yelled.

"Allow me to introduce myself. I'm PJ, your clothes hamper," the deep voice said.

"What are you doing in my hamper?"

"I'm not in it. I am it. Gee, what a bimbo."

Melissa began to relax a little. This strange creature didn't seem quite as menacing after she thought about it. In fact, the idea seemed humorous.

"This is like a cartoon or a bad movie. How did you get here?"

"You brought me, remember? From that second hand store on Elm. I thought you were smarter than that."

"Of course, I remember. You had this quaint charm that went with the rest of the bedroom set."

"Look, lady, I understand. I've been trying to overcome the stigma of furniture my whole life."

"Can you move or fly around the room, and stuff?"

"Did you stop going to school after third grade? I'm inanimate. Maybe you've seen too many cartoons. It's really simple, and goes like this. I don't move, I don't reveal myself to others, I don't perform on stage, I do not do interviews, and will not speak to reporters. I have not been sent by aliens, I do not have a massage from any divine being, I cannot save the world, and

I'm not your private guardian angel with wings to fly around and help you with your personal problems. And by the way, what the hell is this sick color you've painted me?" PJ's voice had risen until the window rattled.

"It's mauve to match the towels in the bath. And don't change the subject."

"I wouldn't think of doing that, princess, but what the hell were we talking about anyway?"

Melissa found the golf club, wrapped her fingers around the carbon graphite filament shaft, and shook it at the hamper sitting against the wall. "Does this bring it back to mind? Remember? I might beat your brains out for messing up my room every day." She reached down; to one of many articles of clothing that littered the room, and picked up a blouse she'd warn two days ago.

"Oh, that"

"Yes, can you explain yourself?"

"Yes. But be careful with the club."

"Why?"

"You could kill a guy with that thing."

"That's the whole idea. Now what's with my clothes?"

"I eat the odors from dirty clothes for nourishment."

"Yuck. That's gross," she said, making a disgusting face and stepping back. After a moment she realized she still held the blouse, and flung it away.

"It's better than that processed, fat dripping, body clogging, toxic waste you eat."

"I'll have you know I eat very healthy food."

"Yeah? What about that pizza stain I saw on your jeans last Tuesday?" Melissa said nothing. "Ouch," said PJ, "that must have struck home."

"You're changing the subject again," she finely said. "Why are my clothes scattered all over the room?"

"I'm not trying to get you off track. You seem very capable of doing that all by your self."

"The clothes," she screamed, raising the club over her head.

"Remember I said I eat the odors. I have a delicate stomach. I just can't abide the stringy little things you woman wear. And your odor makes me sick, so I threw up."

"That's disgusting."

"You certainly are."

Melissa stormed out of the room. What could she do? She felt like a fool arguing with furniture.

* * *

She stopped putting her clothes in PJ, but left him in the bedroom. On Monday morning she had just stepped out of the shower, and started going through her chest of drawers.

"Are you looking for your blue panties?"

"Yes."

"You wore them last week. They're still dirty."

Melissa realized that she stood in front of PJ naked, and frantically tried to cover herself.

"Hay, don't bother. Believe me as a clothes hamper I've seen everything. Boy, could I tell you stories. I even stayed in a burlesque house for a while. Some of the worst indigestion I've ever had. And, of course, I almost starved to death at the nudist colony."

"Why you, self centered, egotistical piece of wicker. Is that all you can think about—your stomach?"

"Well, I'm very hungry. I haven't had a decent meal in a long time. Say, why don't you get a boyfriend, and maybe I could get a decent pair of shorts to chew on. Or how about some wet cardboard? I can get drunk on that odor."

Again she stormed out of the room. How dare he bring up her problems?

* * *

Later that week, while putting on her makeup, Melissa heard a noise. She cautiously stepped out of the bathroom. A man stood at the doorway of her bedroom. Panic overcame her. He wore a ski mask and held a knife. He stood between her and the golf clubs.

"What have we here?" He said in a sick menacing tone.

She tried to scream as he lunged toward her, but she remained frozen. Everything seemed to happen in slow motion. She saw the hamper moved forward, tipping into the path of the intruder.

The man's foot caught, knees buckled, balance lost, his head went crashing into the night stand. The unconscious form lay at Melissa's feet. She quickly removed the mask to reveal the creepy guy who lived down the hall. Then she noticed PJ.

The man had crushed in the side of the hamper. A large rip ran across the front with many wicker strands torn. The lid had been broken off, and the base cracked.

"PJ, are you all right?"

"No," he answered in a weak voice.

"What can I do?" she said, trying to move him out from under the man's leg.

"I don't know. Call the police first. He may wake up any time."

After the police had taken the intruder away, taken her statement, and did all the details of their job, it had been hours. She ran back to PJ, and carefully tried to reassemble him. The pieces didn't quite fit.

"PJ, are you okay? Talk to me. Please talk to me."

He said nothing.

She used her glue gun and duct tape the best she could. It didn't seem to help. After three days the wicker started to crumble to the touch. Also an odor became apparent, and not a good one. What could she do?

* * *

She walked through the sand carrying the cardboard box. The low sun and cool breeze from the ocean told Melissa that twilight would engulf her within the hour. She found the concrete circle on the beach and opened the box. Removing the bottle, breaking the seal, and taking a long drink, set her in the right frame of mind.

"Here's to you PJ. Thank you. I wished I could have done more." She poured the tequila over the box containing the remains of PJ.

"Are you crazy, lady?" A passing bum said. "You could get rid of some of that my way."

"Scram."

She stopped with two inches left in the bottle and took another drink. A match easily set it all a blaze in the bonfire pit. Sitting in the sand, she watched the flames and the sunset. She toasted the fire with her last drink.

"I hope you find an NBA locker room in the sky. And you were wrong, PJ. You were my guardian angle. Here's to earning your wings."

END

AUTHORS COMMENTS

Yes, I brought back PJ. And who wouldn't? The one thing that struck me was his (it's?) sexism. I think it has more to do with tummy issues then with gender. I think he (it) makes up for it in the end.

Come to think of it, I'm not really sure what gender a hamper is.

LITTLE DARK SPOT

Hector moved his horse onto the bridge. He always thought these bridges as useless. They went from one side of nowhere to another. Who would build such a beautiful structure simply to cross the path? If you wanted to get to the other side of the road, walk across it. The people in the time before the nano-tech meltdown were stupid. When technology went away, so did the insanity.

Quickly dismounting, he joined his lieutenant at the railing of the only elevation on the valley floor. In opposite directions in the distance, the feet of the mountains lurked behind the morning fog, giants watching the small dramas unfolding between them.

"Right where you said it would be." His lieutenant handed him the beat-up, field glasses.

After removing his gloves, he put the binoculars to his eyes and focused. The village was smaller then he had expected. Just as well, they had never ventured this far south into the San Joaquin before. He liked the warmer climate. It agreed with him. Perhaps he should have paid more attention to the birds. They were seeking a new summer.

"Look to the left. There's a stand of N-tech power trees. We're in for a little comfort," the lieutenant said, unable to hide his excitement.

"Perhaps lights and running water. We could use a bath," Hector said almost to himself. "This feels good. Maybe we'll stay a while. Hit some of the villages further south." He lowered the binoculars and took in a deep breath of autumn. He loved a raid in the crisp morning air. They were always successful.

"Mount up," he snapped, not taking his eyes off the misty settlement in the distance.

The lieutenant got on his horse, galloped down the slope of the bridge, and joined the rest of his band. Sounds of loading equipment and the checking of weapons soon followed.

Into each life a little darkness. Hector smiled, feeling no compassion for the peasants in the village. They were the herd that grazed on the land. As a predator, he must feed on them.

•

In slow strokes, Patricia moved the brush down the back of her daughter's head.

"Your hair is getting much too long. You'll get it tangled on your long nose."

"No, it isn't."

"Yes. I think we should whack it off about here." Making her fingers into the shape of scissors, she grabbed an ample lock at ear level. "Then we could feed it to the crows."

"No," Jenny protested, "that would make me ugly." She pulled away and faced her mother. They both smiled.

Patricia hugged her. "You'll always be beautiful to me."

With a crash and a twang from the rusty spring the screen door of their home flung open. Storming into the bedroom, her husband Jon removed his work jacket.

"Visitors are approaching from the west," he stated. Sliding his arms into his good dark blue coat, he paused and admired his family.

"I think Jenny should play somewhere else," he said, adjusting his collar. He gave a small gesture with his head toward the back of the house.

Patricia understood. You had to be cautious with strangers. Most were travelers and traders, but others brought trouble.

"Come on Jenny. Get your dolly. Let's play in the basement."

After she persuaded her daughter to stay busy by herself, Patricia latched the door to the cellar and made her way to the common in the center of the town. Others were already milling around watching. As the constable, Jon stood with the mayor. A touch of pride always came to her when he did his official duties. He had earned the people's trust and respect, despite his youth.

She caught sight of him as the riders approached ahead of their dust. There were half a dozen horsemen and a large wagon covered with canvas. They rode across the viaduct bridge and into the common.

"Welcome to Tranquility," the mayor said in a loud clear voice. "What is your business?"

"To take from simple folk like you. We've been raiding towns, up north, and have decided to enjoy what you have to offer."

"You can't do that," Jon protested. He reached into his coat and pulled out a white cloth with a sold black circle in the center. "This is our only defense."

The tall rider removed a revolver from his belt and shot him.

Jon stumbled backwards.

"NO," Patricia screamed, as she started toward her husband. Arms reached out and grabbed her. A safety net of neighbors held her back. All she could see was his form lying in the dirt. Time stopped. The image of him clutching his chest burned into her memory. She jolted back to reality when she heard another shot. The mayor slumped to the ground.

"My name is Hector," the horseman shouted at the stunned villagers. Riders from his group circled the common, and others with rifles jumped out from the wagon. Off in the distance, fresh clouds of dust were raised by more horses. "We'll be staying for a while. If you do what you're told, you'll see the spring."

Patricia collapsed to her knees, tears flooding her face.

•

She stared at the draped body of her dead husband. She couldn't remember coming to the barn on the other side of the power trees. Grief had locked her in time. A kind neighbor draped a shawl over her shoulders.

"You need to stay warm, dear."

Patricia couldn't even say, thank you. Her thoughts drifted to where she and Jon had met. Jon had traveled south, to Oil Field, on business. This was the place where she grew up. She showed him the pit the meltdown had made of two cities. The evil workings of man had left deep scars and chaos. People who survived the brief fury of techno-destruction could only stand and gape.

He had kissed her for the first time on a clear warm evening. Then Jon asked her to dwell with him in Tranquillity. It had been such a happy moment in her life. Her husband and Jenny were all she had in the world. Now chaos had returned and ripped another pit, this time through her heart.

She began to be aware of the other people in the barn and other bodies. Four covered and lifeless mounds already looked like earth in the dim light filtering through the cracks between the vertical boards. The mayor's wife leaned forward, sobbing next to her husband.

A man named Blake entered the barn. Patricia had never cared much for him, but he represented what remained of the leadership of the town.

"They've taken over the hall. So no school or Sunday services," he said to the small group. He took a moment, and gently touched Patricia's shoulder. "My wife is with Jenny. She'll be all right," he said softly.

"What are they going to do?" the mayor's brother asked.

"We've all heard about the raiding parties up north along the Sacramento. That's where this bunch came from. They've decided to stay here until spring. That could be three, maybe four months."

"Isn't there anything we can do?" one of the women asked.

"We can't fight them," said Ted, Patricia's neighbor. "The first thing they did was to take away our few shotguns. And there are just too many. I counted sixteen."

Patricia always thought of Ted as a coward.

"Didn't Miguel have a pistol?" another asked.

"They got it."

"We can't escape. They've put guards on the road and the water tower. They can watch everyone." Ted continued to annoy Patricia.

"We can't expect help from other towns," Blake said, reasserting control over the discussion. "They haven't the weapons or skills to overrun them. The situation is intolerable. Before three months are done, we'll be murdered trying to defend ourselves or starving with all our food gone."

"What can we do?" cried from a woman in the back.

"I've talked with most of the others. There is an action we can take, although a drastic one."

Patricia looked up at Blake and the others, all dark silhouettes in front of thin bright lines of the afternoon sun coming through the barn. Dust danced in the air as the light sliced through the blackness.

"We can deny them the taking of our lives."

A murmur spread through the group. Patricia couldn't believe the situation was that desperate. Her stomach felt even sicker. Were they really willing to elevate this to madness?

"We can take away from them the one thing they came here for."

"Are you talking about mass death?"

"That's right. What else is there for us to do? If we do nothing, we're dead. We can deny them the killing. It's the only way we have to strike back."

Some began to argue. Many wanted to express their opinions.

"You can't seriously want more lives taken after what's happened? Think of our children," Patricia insisted.

"Who knows what horrible thing will happen to them if we don't."

The debate continued back and forth. But Blake had a convincing way about him. In the end the others agreed.

"I have what we need right here," Blake said, holding up a small envelope. "Most of the others already have theirs." He opened the flap and moved around to each person.

Blake stopped in front of Patricia and held out his large open hand holding many small folded pieces of rice paper.

"I can't do it," she said, and turned her head away.

"You don't have a choice. It's one kind of death or another. Please, don't let it be by our hands."

Everyone knew what he meant but his honesty shocked her. She hesitated, but took two of the tiny packets, and held them tight in her fist. Her mind filled with hate and fear at being forced into this. She couldn't stay there any longer and needed to find Jenny, the one thing that still made sense.

As she walked away from the barn and approached the small grove she stopped in front of the newest power tree. It hadn't been there when she first arrived in Tranquility with Jon. She had watched it grow over the years with the realization that the increase in demand for energy was partly due to her and Jenny.

It loomed over her head. Each blue, hand-size hexagon leaf moved and shifted to find the maximum amount of sunlight. Every step she took creaked from the sound of crushing the soft carbon buds that lay under the tree. Like strange fruit they formed under the leaves then fall to the ground, their use and purpose forgotten.

The nano-machines moving inside the smooth gray bark transformed material from the ground, water and air to provide and store power for the village. If more was needed, a runner from one tree would poke up from the ground and start another.

If everyone died would the trees stop growing? Would they get smaller and retreat back into the earth? Would the tiny machines make all the trees disappear? Having no masters to serve, would they also die?

●

Hector and his lieutenant walked in the shade of the artificial trees and came upon a young woman with her back to them. She had dark shoulder-length hair and wore a simple blue cotton dress. Their approach startled her. She spun around to face them and reacted by bringing her fist to her chest.

"Murderer," she accused.

"You shot her husband this morning," was whispered in Hectors' ear.

"Don't be frightened. I'm sorry about the death in your family. Nothing personal, you understand. I just needed to gain dominance and control."

"You're an animal," she said, her eyes burning into him, "with a wicked heart."

"I'm no different from you."

"You have a black soul."

"Don't be so pompous." He was amused at her fearlessness. "You and your friends are not as righteous as you let on. That soul of yours has a dark spot of its own. Little bits of ugliness that would make you wither and die if other people knew what they were."

"You're wrong. I could never have done the merciless acts you committed. No one in this village could."

"You're mistaken. I've seen it in others. All are capable. Most of you bottle it up, hide it and don't understand what you have in you. But the blackness is there. On the other hand, I'm not afraid of who I am. Letting it run wild is what I do." He took a step in her direction.

Hector watched as terror seemed to overpower her and she ran toward the center of the village.

"I may have to console that young widow," Hector said, turning to his lieutenant, "one of these dark and chilly nights. Show her I'm not such a bad guy." They laughed and continued on their way.

•

Patricia thanked Blake's wife for staying with Jenny. Her heart still raced from the encounter with Hector. She sat on the bed and watched her sleeping daughter's quiet breathing.

Opening her fist, she looked at the instruments of destruction. Was her heart as black as Hector's? Could she go through with this? How could she not? If only Jon were here to help her. Death or death— the symmetry made it easy. She unwrapped the top square and looked at the small black dot in the center. Undoing the top three buttons of her dress, she peeled off the dark patch from the rice paper, and pressed it to the soft skin between her breasts.

Tears filled her eyes as she remembered gentle words and nestling with her husband. This was so hard to do without him. She knew it must be done quickly if she were to get through it.

She unwrapping the other paper, peeled off the dot, and turned to Jenny—hands tucked under her chin, eyes closed, a face the envy of angels. Gently moving the child's arm away from her body, Patricia placed the patch on her daughter's chest.

This was more than she could take and she began to sob. Pulling herself onto the bed, she held Jenny close.

"Mommy?"

"It's all right, dear. Go to sleep." Patricia's tears continued to flow.

Although she couldn't feel it, she knew tiny machines were entering her body through the skin. They said it would be painless, with no sensation. She felt tired and exhausted, knowing it wouldn't be quick.

She must have dozed off.

Bad dreams woke her. Where was Jenny? Feeling dizzy, weak and sick, she tried to call her daughter's name. Her throat wouldn't work. Getting out of bed, she stumbled into the bathroom. Jenny wasn't there. She couldn't see her.

Steadying herself at the sink, she looked in the mirror, but couldn't focus. A grey splotch fluttered in front of her eyes, and they throbbed. Dizziness overcame her, and she collapsed on the floor.

•

Hector twisted the knob on the homemade arc lamp. A carbon rod came in contact with another, and a sizzling sound announced the light.

"That's better than candles," Hector said. The dark paneled walls reflected little of the harsh light as it filled the room. The tables and chairs in the hall were empty and pushed to one side. Except for the ones where Hector sat with his lieutenant. They ate roasted chicken, taken from a house across the common.

"Everything went well today," said the lieutenant, chewing on a wing.

"Yes, it did. Be sure to tell everyone I'm pleased."

"Already have."

"Good. And what about our hosts? Have they been as cooperative as you expected?"

"They've been very quiet this evening. I expected much more resistance. It's not like these earthy farmers to take it lying down."

"Just be thankful they're sheep, not bears," Hector said, wiping chicken grease from his chin. "Do you remember that woman we saw this afternoon?"

"You mean the looker, out by the trees?"

"Yeah. She said I'm a terrible person." Hector watched his companion put down his food. The bright point source of light plunged one side of his puzzled expression into deep shadow.

"Do you think I'm a bad person?" Hector asked.

The lieutenant snapped upright and placed his hand on his chest. "My word heavens no. You've always treated me well."

They both burst into laughter, unable to maintain a straight face. Hector almost choked on a bit of bird. Their amusement came to a quick halt as a shot erupted from the darkness.

"What was that?" They both jumped up.

"Guards are posted. Everyone should be bedded down for the night," the lieutenant said.

One of Hectors men burst through the entrance, his face holding an unholy fear. As soon as he stepped in he was jerked off his feet and back out the door. His screams filled the air with panic.

"Go circle around from the rear," Hector said, "I'll check out front."

The lieutenant disappeared. Hector stepped over to the chair where his gun belt hung and pulled out his revolver. He heard screams coming from behind the building. Animal-like noises began to drift in from all directions of the night. The shrieks and howling were so piercing; he barely heard the front door open again.

The ugly creature walked upright, defying all logic applied to animals. Hector froze in absolute terror. It had maudlin red skin, leathery with small white bumps stretched over long bony limbs. Its narrow sickle claws were in constant twitching motion as it moved toward Hector. The large mouth had short sharp teeth with two long pointed fangs protruding past the lower jaw.

Then the stench of vomited rot hit him, making his stomach wrench.

Where in hell did you come from?

The red eyes of the beast bored into him. He'd seen that thrusting stare before. A mountain lion, just before it leapt onto an unsuspecting doe. Hector had nightmares about that look. It woke him screaming in the dark. He wished he could forget them.

He pulled the hammer back on the pistol. "Get the hell out of here, abomination," Hector commanded.

Terrifying screams continued to drift in from the outside. The situation turned worse. A smaller creature, no more then a meter high entered and moved to Hectors left in the same stalking manner. The drooling and quivering creatures didn't notice each other.

He didn't know which one to shoot first but decided the larger one would be more dangerous. As he raised the weapon, the beast hissed. The stench of hatching maggots overwhelmed him. With a trembling hand, Hector pulled the trigger. He was too slow and the shot went wild. The creatures tackled him, one from each side, pinning his arms. His gun flew across the room.

The jaws of the large one clamped onto his throat, the fangs sank in slowly. The thing was powerful. Hector wondered why it didn't just snap his neck. Mercy was not on his side. Pain and suffering would be made to last.

Then the little creature hopped onto his stomach and ripped at his clothes. Hector freed his arm and tried to strike it. But the beast grabbed his wrist and held it like a twig. Scalpel sharp claws danced down the center of his chest. Stinging agony followed.

He could feel the vampire's coarse tongue shredding his skin as it lapped up the crimson liquid at his neck pumping out his artery.

The little one reached into his ribs. Hector stopped screaming, no longer able to suck air through his mouth. It must have punctured his lungs.

But that wasn't what the creature was after.

•

Patricia slowly opened her eyes. She was cold, wet and naked, lying in the empty bathtub. Her legs were wobbly as she got up and dried herself. Her memories of the day before became clear. At least she thought they did. She relived the loss of her husband but didn't have time to weep. The last thing she remembered was looking for Jenny. Patricia started to dress, and then stopped. Carefully peeling off the small black patch, she placed it back onto the little square of rice paper. The hideous machines were finished this time and she mustn't let the sun go down on that darkness again.

She threw on some clothes. Then she ran outside into the late afternoon sunlight toward the common, calling Jenny's name. Patricia found her standing in front of the hall looking through the open doors.

Blake and another man came out carrying Hectors body. Patricia had to turn away and diverted Jenny's stare. His blood-covered carcass had a large gaping hole in the chest. The men carried the remains to a wagon, and piled it on top of another. This scene was repeated all over the town.

Patricia got on her knees and pulled her daughter close.

"Mommy, did we do that?"

"No darling, of course not," she replied, but could not hide her feelings or deny what she knew. More had happened that night than she wanted to admit. There would be no easy way to explain the truth.

"Well, not exactly. You see, dear, there is a little dark and ugly spot in all of us."

•

END

AUTHORS COMMENTS

Dracula stories are very popular. I just couldn't get away from the SiFi aspect. So I turned vampires into a weapon. A very personal defensive weapon, that only happens at night. Of course one vampire couldn't see another. It would be like looking into a mirror. If they could see another, they would go off and kill each other. That wouldn't be good, at least not in this story.

A TRIP ON THE STEPPE

The small blaze crackled as the aroma of searing meat filled the air. A large man with dark hair turned the stick so the flame wouldn't favor one side of the meal. The night air chilled his back but this mindless cooking chore brought him closer to the warmth.

"I can't believe that all you could get was a rabbit," he said to the skinny little man sitting on a log across from the fire. "We will die of starvation on the road before anyone can kill us."

"Well, I tried to get a nice boar, a really fat one. It would have kept even you happy for at least three days."

"And why didn't you invite him for dinner?"

"My arrow missed. Besides it was too far from camp. I could never have dragged him back here."

"For a man who makes his money as an assassin, your skills leave something to be acquired."

"Don't speak ill of me." The short one stood up and took a determined posture. "The bow is not my favorite. I'm a knife man, and there is none better."

"Be calm, my little friend. My weapon is the sword, and I have a much longer reach." His voice conveyed more of a promise than a threat.

"Ha. I didn't recruit you because you can use a sword. No, I got you because you are tall."

"What are you talking about? I hired you because you are short." He stopped turning the spit and stood up so the other man could see his full height.

The tense moment suddenly erupted into laughter.

"That was quite good," the large man said, going back to turning the rabbit.

"Yeah, we both know how we were recruited."

"That might have been a dark figure in the shadows, but the gold coin he gave us for this task was real."

"Yes. And with the promise of ten more when we're done," the little one said, as he sat back down.

"I believe the generous rabbit is ready for us."

The conversation quieted to the ripping of flesh, the smacking of lips and the gnawing of bone. Talk didn't continue until dinner had been picked clean.

"So tell me, why is he called the Universal Ruler?" The small one asked.

"Because he rules the universe, and is more important than you or me."

"So he'll be easy to spot."

"Of course. All we have to do is to look for the guy with all the bodyguards carrying long spears and big swords. That's where we'll find him."

"That doesn't sound encouraging. We'll have to be very careful."

"This is true. Perhaps even sneaky."

"That's a good idea. Maybe we should enter the camp at night, and try not to be seen."

The larger man reached over and knocked the smaller one on the side of the head. He fell backwards off the log. All that could be seen was his feet up in the air. He picked himself up, and rubbed his head.

"What did you do that for?" he asked, climbing back onto his perch.

"Of course, we will not be seen. We're assassins. If they knew we were trying to kill their leader, Genghis Khan, they would decorate their felt tents with our heads."

"Then it's a good idea?"

"Yes, of course."

"Why did you hit me when I had a good idea?"

"You're slow. Now go to sleep my little friend."

"Yeah. I bet I could outrun you any day."

"I can't hear you," the large man said, as he threw a blanket over his body. "I'm asleep."

"I bet I'm even faster asleep that you."

The covering flew off the big man. "Where's my sword?"

"All right. See, I'm lying down."

*   *   *

The next day the large wooden wheels of their old weathered cart slowly turned as they lumbered along the path. The sky had brightened with the lifting of the morning haze. The expansive grassy plain of the Steppes seemed to go on forever, yielding only to the occasional outcropping of rock or stand of trees.

The wagon rounded a bend. A brown cloaked figure further up the road turned around to see them approaching. The mysterious person dashed into the bushes and crept behind a boulder.

"Did you see that?"

"Yes, I did, my little friend."

"Who do you suppose that is?"

"Let's find out. You keep the cart going as if nothing has happened. I'll jump out, and circle to the other side."

As soon as he hit the ground he quickly moved to the far side of the rock, and snuck unnoticed up behind the figure watching the cart moving slowly down the path. He grabbed the person by the arm and pulled the hood back. It revealed a dark haired young woman with large almond eyes, smooth skin and good teeth.

The smaller man ran back to join them.

"Why are you hiding from us?" the tall one asked.

"Because, you're big and ugly."

"This makes sense," the skinny one said.

"Where are you going and what is your name?"

"I'm on my way to see my younger sister. Our father died, and I have no other place to go. She is in the court of Genghis Khan. I'm known as Kim"

"We're going in that direction. I think you should travel with us."

"And why is that?"

"For mutual protection. These roads can be dangerous. You never know what kinds of people are traveling on them."

"Are you afraid of robbers? Do you two need my protection?" she asked with a smirk on her face.

"I think not," the little one spoke up. "But you would be wise to travel with a group. You don't know what kind of unspeakable fate you might find."

"My half-sized friend is right. We could protect you from dangerous people."

"And how will I be safe from the two of you?"

"We will watch each other," the small one said, with a smile.

"Oh, that does make me feel much better."

* * *

As the woman prepared the fire, the small man beckoned the other away. Stars filled the sky, and the familiar cold wind joined them by the horse.

"This is very fortunate for us."

"How is that?" asked the large man.

"We can enter the town during the day, and won't have to sneak around."

"I can tell you have a thought in that ugly head of yours. Just say it. What do you have in mind?"

"Don't you see what an opportunity this is?"

"Do you mean getting her to cook your scrawny rabbits?"

"No. While she is with us, we appear to have a reason to be in the camp. The only thing better would be if we had some children."

"I'll keep an eye out for any along the road."

"Don't you get it? A family is less threatening than two rough guys like us alone."

"I see what you're saying. But what I picked up is the fact that she has a sister in the court. If we're going to kill Khan, this could be of great value."

"What about my sister?"

Both men jumped and turned around to find the woman carrying a handful of twigs approaching them. It was a slow race to see which one would regain his composure first.

"What my tall friend is trying to say is that we also have business at the court of Genghis Khan. And this is a very good opportunity because we don't have anyone to present us."

"So you want my sister to help you? And why would she do this?"

"Because we are protecting you on this journey. And she should be very appreciative of that."

"I'm wandering through this dark and dangerous forest heavily burdened with firewood, and you two are talking to the horse." She waved the small sticks in front of their noses. "I don't think my sister would favor you well if she heard about this."

"What are you talking about? There is but a handful of trees."

"Nevertheless, it will require more."

"What do you want?" The tall man resigned himself to the outcome. She had a look he had seen before in other women. He would lose the argument, and she would get her way.

"Give me a gold coin. Each of you. In advance."

"What are you saying? I won't do it. She is the thief on this road," yelled the little man. He became as animated as he was vociferous, waving his arms and making a racket.

"Let me talk with my ugly friend," the tall one said, as he pulled the ranting man away from her. He leaned in to whisper.

"I say we give her the coins."

"How did you get crazy talking drunk without me knowing about it?"

"I haven't been drinking. I'm serious. We don't have a choice. We'll need to pay her."

"Maybe you hit your head? We don't need her. We can do just fine by ourselves."

"No, my little friend. Getting an introduction from her sister will greatly increase our chances of success. Without it, we could lose the ten gold coins and our lives. We must take this chance."

"All right, but if this doesn't help us, and we get killed anyway, then we'll do things my way."

"Agreed."

They turned around and found her hand cupped to her ear, trying to listen. She quickly removed it.

"My little friend and I will each give you a coin."

"Good," she said, turning to leave. But she hesitated. "Ugly friend, tall one. I wish you two would learn each other's names. It would make things a lot easier." She made her way back to the fire, the two men carefully watching her.

"Do you think we ought to tell her our names?" The little man asked.

"No. We agreed not to tell each other, in case one of us is caught. If it annoys her, that's fine with me. If she has taken our money, she now works for us, and will do what we say."

* * *

Felt tents, smoke from cooking fires, horses and the movement of a thousand people carpeted the shallow valley floor. Activities of every kind that accompanied such a large gathering of people could be seen. The aromas from the livestock and cooking fires drifted on the breeze as they moved the cart closer to the royal encampment.

They passed by a large open field circled by mounted horses of every color and size. The riders took turns galloping their steeds and shooting arrows at an overturned basket as they passed.

"They are very good with a bow," the little one said.

"Yes, they wouldn't have missed a three-day sized boar. We must be very careful."

They found a place to stop, and jumped down from the cart.

"You two stay here," the woman said. "I'll go find my sister. If we can set up an audience with Khan right away, I'll send someone to get you. If we can't, I'll be back to tell you myself."

She stood in front of the two men with her hand out. She smiled. They each put a gold coin into her palm. Turning, she walked toward the royal tents.

"This is awfully soon. I hope you have a plan because we're not ready," the small one said.

"Do not worry. Hide your knife. We'll tell them we have important news about a threat to the Khan. When we're presented, I'll grab him. You will cut him deep. Then we'll defend ourselves from the guards. After that, we slip out the back of the tent to blend in with all these others." He made a sweep with his hand to show the encampment.

"That's a good plan."

"Thank you." He knew they were taking a terrible chance. But the thought of ten gold coins made it bearable.

"What if it doesn't work?"

"The price for failure remains the same as when we took on this job."

"And what is that?"

"Death."

"We must be very careful."

The large man wanted to reach over and smack him on the head. But now was not the time. They were waiting for the most important moment in their lives.

* * *

Genghis Khan stroked his beard as he sat cross-legged on a large wooden chest draped with animal skins. He wore only a pair of dark silk breeches embroidered with gold. A large guard approached, dipping his head with the usual formalities.

"My Khan, one of the concubines requests an audience. She has brought someone who claims to have information of great importance."

"Bring them."

The girl was not his favorite, but he wouldn't get rid of her either. She had another woman, dressed in peasant clothes, with her.

"My Khan, this is my older sister, Kim who has arrived from the north. She has an account of her journey you must hear."

The woman stepped forward with no hesitation.

"During my travel, I had the opportunity to discover two men who are planning to kill you this very day."

Genghis Khan jumped up from the wooden chest. The one thing he hated worse then an arrogant king who wouldn't pay his tribute was an attack on his life.

"Guard, send for your captain. And you, you will tell me every detail."

"Yes, my Khan."

*   *   *

The two sisters made their way between the felt tents. The long day came down to a walk near sunset. The air had cooled, but the camps' activity had not lessened.

"That's disturbing," the older sister said, as she stopped and looked up.

"Yes, it is," the younger one replied. She saw the heads of the two would-be assassins stuck on poles.

"It's a gruesome business to deal with the criminals you found."

"I don't mean that. They are now the same height. I hired one because he was tall and the other because he was short. That way, they would be easier to spot and point out."

"You sent these men to kill Genghis Khan?"

She nodded with a smile. "I recruited them separately as I hid in dark shadows."

"But why?"

"By exposing them, we obtained The Khan's favor. Are we not better off now then we were before? He is very thankful and has already made our lives better."

"What if it went wrong? We could be up there."

"Sometimes we must take a dangerous chance to secure our future. I'm sure they would have agreed."

The heads did not reply.

END

AUTHORS COMMENTS

This story started out as a self-imposed exercise. What if you had two guys were sitting around a camp fire. Who are they, what are they and what are they going to do? From there this story emerged.

In my subsequent research into Genghis Khan I found out that he died of falling off a horse. This is such irony because the Mongols were considered the best horseman in the world at that time.

I knew from the start that my two assassins would never succeed.

ABOUT THE AUTHOR

Ryan Robinson was Quality Manager of a small high tech company in Southern California. He has degrees in electronics and computer science; disciplines include looking at what happened in the past to see events in the future. His duties included writing procedures and technical documents. Now retired, he gets to write for fun. A love of history, science, and what makes people tick inspire his stories.

One reviewer said, "I was immediately struck by the unusual imagination and technical texture in his stories, fiction and science fiction."

He has been writing for many years and *The Curse of Tecumseh* is his first book.

ABOUT THE BOOK

Did the Shawnee military leader, Tecumseh, put a curse on America? Can furniture be heroic? Who really is your best friend? How do you survive in the future nano-tech dystopia? Is it hard to talk to a fire lizard? Answers to these and other questions can be found in these stories. The names have been changed to protect the innocent. The guilty, on the other hand, will have to fend for themselves.

Some authors discover that writing short stories is a good way to start their journey and learn the craft. This collection is a result of such a journey. These stories will take you far afield in fact and fiction in both time and space.

Printed in the USA
CPSIA information can be obtained
at www.ICGtesting.com
LVHW011402141223
766290LV00076B/1876